OUR STORIES

HOPE'S ARRIVAL

THE NATIVITY THROUGH THEIR EYES

DEBORAH GATCHEL

CORPUS CHRISTI, TX

First edition

ISBN 978-0-9963995-3-1 (Paperback)

ISBN 978-0-9963995-4-8 (Hardback)

Interior art © Christina Gatchel https://www.Artistree.io/christallized

Cover image by Virtually Possible Designs https://www.VirtuallyPossibleDesigns.com/

Published by Eternity Imprints https://www.EternityImprints.com/

Contents

And the Word became
flesh and dwelt among us,
and we beheld His glory,
the glory as of the only
begotten of the Father,
full of grace and truth.
John 1:14

Our Stories

HOPE'S ARRIVAL

Contents

Introduction

For six years in the early 2000s, I spent every summer in Ghana, West Africa. Along with the amazing friends and adopted family there, I gained an appreciation for the culture. One thing that struck me was the parallels between Ghanaian and ancient Israelite cultures.

One aspect I noticed, in particular, was their care for the outsider. As a *bruni* (white person) in Ghana, I could show up in any village and have a place to stay and food to eat. They would give me their last grains of rice and sleep outside in the rain before turning me away.

Middle Eastern cultures have the same hospitality requirements. It was true in Abraham's time and still holds true today. As I thought about this parallel, I could not mesh this picture with the common, Western portrayal of the first Christmas. I didn't know how to verify the accuracy so, I prayed for wisdom.

Days later, I ran across an article titled "Born in a Manger but not in a Stable." The author presented cultural and linguistic details that gave me a stepping stone to begin my studies.

It's been an amazing journey. I invite you to join me.

First, let's set out some travel guidelines.

1. The Bible is our ultimate guide to Truth. We can trust what is found on its pages.

2. As we read the Bible, we must interpret it within the culture in which it was written. In 2000 years, many traditions have crept in to color our understanding of the Bible. We must separate those traditions from Truth and set them aside if a more accurate picture is required by the text or context.

With these guidelines established, let's go.

What does the Bible tell us about the birth of Christ? Reading Luke 2, we know:

- Jesus was born of a virgin.
- Mary and Joseph were both righteous.
- Cesar Augustus issued a decree that the whole world should be registered for taxation.
- Joseph was of the house and lineage of David, so he went to Bethlehem to be registered.
- Mary went with him.
- While they were in Bethlehem, the time came for the baby to be born.
- They wrapped Him in swaddling clothes and laid him in a manger.
- There was no room for them in the common lodging area.

What the Bible does not say:

- The Bible does not tell us where Joseph was born nor where he lived.

- The Bible does not tell us that they skidded into town with Mary transitioning into second-stage labor, crying as Joseph knocked on the door of multiple inns trying to find a place to deliver the baby. It makes for a good story, but it does not fit with "**while they were there, the time came** for her to be delivered," nor with the hospitality-focused culture.

- And, please stay with me, the Bible does not say Mary and Joseph were cast off in a dirty stable to navigate the birthing process alone as first-time parents.

But, what about no room in the inn and being laid in a manger?

I'm glad you asked. To answer that question, let's first take a look at a standard Jewish home.

Four-Room House

Archaeologists have identified what they call the four-room Israelite house. It first shows up in the material culture about the time the Hebrews moved into Canaan, and it became the classic home in the area until the time of the exile. Many archeologists will classify a site as Israelite based on the presence of such homes. After the Jews returned from exile in Babylon, the layout changed slightly, but the basic components remained the same.

The home is structured in a U shape, consisting of four rooms: The main courtyard in the center of the U, long rooms along the left and right walls, and one long, wide room along the back. Any of these rooms may or may not be divided into additional rooms either by pillars, sheets, or actual walls. One or both of the side rooms were dedicated to housing the cows, donkeys, and other valuable or sick livestock. Farm equipment, grains, oils, and other food stores were kept in the back room. The courtyard was used for daily activities such as cooking, eating, grinding grain, pressing oil, spinning, and weaving.[1]

Often, a second story was built above the backroom creating a single, large upstairs room. Whether single- or two-story, stairs led to the roof with a banister around the edge. The family would sleep on the roof on warm summer nights.

Absent from the Jewish housing complex was a separate stable for animals; they were kept in the room off the courtyard where they could be protected from thieves.

Tax System

Now let's take a look at the Roman tax system. The Romans levied heavy taxes to pay for the army and many building programs. When the Senate called for a tax, individuals (tax farmers) could bid for the job of collecting said taxes. Whoever promised to collect the highest amount won the bid, and then would conduct a census, requiring everyone to register their property in order to assess their tax liability. The tax farmers would up-charge the citizens to line their own pockets. Caesar Augustus (the first Roman Emperor, r. 27 BC-14 AD) began the slow process of reforming the tax system to relieve the corruption. It was under this system that Joseph had to return to Bethlehem to register his family's land.

No room, where?

Now that we understand the historical and cultural context a little better, let's go back to the story.

Most English translations tell us that Mary laid Jesus in a manger because there was no room in **the inn**. Let's take a look at this crowded location.

There are two Greek words that might be translated "inn". The first one, *pandocheion*, clearly means a public inn for travelers. Luke uses this word when he tells the story of the Good Samaritan (Luke 10:25-37).

The other word that might be translated "inn" is *kataluma*. It was used for any type of accommodation – an open-air khan, a public guest house, or the upstairs room of the four-room house. This is the word Luke uses when he tells us where Jesus and the disciples had the Last Supper (Luke 22:7-38). This is also how he describes the place that was full when Jesus was born (Luke 2:7).

Bethlehem was a small town when Jesus was born. Archaeologists place the population between 300 and 1000 people. It was on a major highway so it probably had a single, open-air, khan-style inn run by a shopkeeper who could provide food and other necessities for a fee.

So, let's piece this all together.

- The Jews of Jesus' day did not know of a separate stable. Their animals were kept in the house just off the courtyard. That is where we would expect to find the manger.

- Middle Eastern hospitality required homeowners to take in travelers, especially a young couple expecting a baby.

- Luke used both terms for inn in his Gospel, but he used *kataluma* to describe the place that was full at Jesus's birth and the room where Jesus ate the Last Supper.

I propose, based on the work of a growing number of Bible-believing scholars, that our Western understanding of the nativity is culturally improbable.

Mary and Joseph weren't turned away from multiple inns, or even one. They likely arrived weeks, or even months before Jesus was born. Then, with so many family members returning to Bethlehem to register their property for taxation, the guest room was full. The quietest place for Mary to deliver the baby would have been the stable room, right off the courtyard. Rather than being cast aside to navigate the birth by herself, Mary gave birth in the home, surrounded by family and supported with love.

Does our understanding of this cultural tidbit make a difference to our salvation?

Not at all. The Gospel is clear: "Believe in the Lord Jesus Christ and you will be saved" (Acts 16:31). "For God so loved the world that He gave His only begotten son that whosoever believes in Him shall not perish but have eternal life" (John 3:16). None of the salvation verses require belief in any particular account of Christ's birth.

But, when we cast Jesus aside in the stable, His birth becomes strange and unrelatable. We also introduce improbabilities that cast doubt on the reliability of Scripture – questions that disappear when we have an accurate understanding.

Let's bring Him out of the stable, into a loving home, surrounded by friends and family. Let's let the Christmas story make sense.

For a more detailed examination of the Biblical, historical, and cultural details of Luke 2, please the blog series, "A Way in a Manger" at HopesArrival.com.

---

1. A model of a typical Israelite house, the so-called four-room house. Image: Nick Laarakkers at nl.wikipedia - Own work. CC BY-SA 3.0

Zechariah

I TRACE THE LETTERS of my name on the lot tile. Zechariah. "The Lord remembers."

Does He remember me? With no heir to carry my name, I will surely be cast off and forgotten.

I drop my lot into the basket and then hand my purity token to the secretary.

He looks at it and smiles. "Still strong enough to pass inspection?"

"The Lord has blessed me with strength to serve Him."

The others chat quietly in the pre-dawn stillness while I move toward the side of the courtyard.

I take in the scene around me. *How many priests through the centuries have stood in this courtyard and prayed for the honor of having their lot drawn?*

Today, though, I pray that I'm not chosen. Ten years ago, my father was gathered to our ancestors. Since the Lord did not bless me with a child, his name will be cut off. *Could there be a greater shame? Anything I offer will be tainted. I should have* held *my lot so I can't be called.*

My old friend Simeon kisses me on the cheek and whispers, "The Messiah is coming soon. In that we have hope."

I smile warmly at him, a true friend who understands grief. "You still haven't found the Messiah? How long has it been since the Lord promised you would see him?"

He shrugs, "One day or fifty years. What does it matter? He Who Promises is faithful. We always have hope." He slips to the back of the crowd with the off-duty priests and the others who have gathered for morning worship. He calls to me again, "We always have hope."

Hope. Maybe. Even if the Lord has forgotten me, surely, He will not forget His people.

The presiding priest draws a lot from the basket. "Cleaning the altar and preparing the fires."

Throw out the waste, just like me. If you must use me today, put me here. But my name is not called.

The machinery churns, filling the basin with water so those chosen to serve can wash their feet. They then wait by the entrance to the Holy Place while the lot is drawn for the morning sacrifice. By the Grace of the Holy One, my name is not drawn.

I watch as the lamb is brought out and presented. At the same time, the priests enter the Holy Place to cleanse the altar of yesterday's incense and trim the lamp wicks.

The birds overhead sing their morning song while we recite the prayers. "With great love You have loved us, O Lord our God, and with much overflowing pity, You have pitied us. For You are a God who prepares salvation, and You have chosen us from among all nations. Blessed be the Lord who in love chose His people Israel."

The Lord Who builds up Jerusalem and gathers the exiles of Israel, Who heals the brokenhearted and binds up their wounds.

You determine the number of the stars and call them each by name. Hear my prayer and cause me to trust You.[1]

"Present the morning incense." The priest reaches into the lot basket again. "Zechariah."

Why today, Lord? I look at the ground and take a deep breath. *Help me to honor You through my grief and shame.*

I choose two of my nephews and wait outside as they pour the coals on the altar and light the lamps. When they leave, I step into the room and place the incense on the altar. *I've completed my task and the Lord didn't strike me down.*

As I walk backward toward the door, movement to the right of the altar catches my attention. *No one should be here.*

Light spreads from a man in the corner and fills the room. My thoughts jumble. *I need to get out of here.* But my feet won't move.

"Zechariah, don't be afraid."

It's more than a command. A blessing of peace floods over me.

"The Lord has heard your prayer. You are not forgotten. Elizabeth will bear you a son. You are to name him John."

A son?

"He will be great in the sight of the Lord and will be filled with the Holy Spirit even before he is born."

The peace that covered me at first scatters with my thoughts as I try to grasp his message.

"He will go before Him in the spirit and power of Elijah, to turn the hearts of the fathers to the children, and the disobedient to the wisdom of the just, to prepare the people for the Lord."

I know all those words. I have recited those prophecies countless times. But here, now, they don't make sense.

"Elizabeth and I are too old. This cannot be. I need a sign!"

The angel seems to grow taller. "I am Gabriel. I stand before the Almighty God. He sent me to deliver this message to you. Here is your sign, you will not be able to speak until all these things are fulfilled."

And, in a moment, he is gone.

Everything goes silent. I can no longer hear the crackling of the coals on the altar. The birds' songs cease. I look around frantically. I am no longer clean. I must retreat from the Holy Presence. I shouldn't even be in the Temple. I back out of the room and turn to face the other priests. But when I try to speak, I cannot form any words. I try again. Nothing.

I'm supposed to lead the benediction.

Finally, I motion to the priest next to me to speak the blessing. I hear the words in my heart of hearts.

"The Lord bless you and keep you." *Elizabeth will bear you a son.*

"The Lord make His face to shine upon you and be gracious to you." *He will be great in the sight of the Lord.*

"The Lord lift up His countenance upon you..." *To prepare the people for the Lord.*

"And give you Peace."[2]

Can it be? Why would the Lord bless me in this way? Will I really have a heritage? Am I no longer cast out?

Bless you and keep you. Be gracious to you. Give you peace. We always have hope. Thank you, Lord! Amen. Amen.

---

1. From Psalm 147:2-4

2. From Numbers 6:24-26

The Lord bless you and keep you;
The Lord make His face shine
upon you, and be gracious to you;
The Lord lift up His countenance
upon you, and give you peace.
Numbers 6:24-26

Mary

I STAND BESIDE PAPA. Joseph shuffles his feet and fiddles with his robe on Papa's other side, but I don't dare look at him.

The lawyer asks, "Does the girl accept the terms?"

Accept the terms? Do I have a choice? Seven years ago, Papa's cousin died. Papa took his son, Joseph, as his apprentice in exchange for my hand in marriage.

"If seven years was good enough for Jacob and Rachel, it's good enough for you," he told me.

Do I accept the terms? For seven years I've watched him diligently work beside Papa. I listened as they discussed the Torah. Even now, though he is still young, he is considered a leader in the synagogue. He is so tender with my sisters' children and always respectful of the elders. *Why do I hesitate?*

Papa wraps his arm around my shoulder. "Do you agree?"

I look into his eyes then bury my head in his chest. *To say yes means I leave the shelter of your arms.*

He kisses the top of my head and whispers, "He's a good man."

I wipe my eyes on his robe then turn to the lawyer. "I agree."

The next few months are a blur of activity as Mamma and I prepare for my wedding. Of course, the normal activities don't stop. We still must cook and clean and continue with the weaving for market. Weaving is my favorite. While I'm lacing the threads through the loom, I have time to think and dream, and, usually, no one will interrupt my work, asking me to fetch water or grind the wheat.

Today, Mamma is at the market and the rest of the girls are at their own homes. I have some rare time to myself. I sit down at the loom and pick up the shuttle.

As I weave, I dream about the days to come. I imagine myself, baby in my arms, serving a beautiful meal to Joseph.

"Peace be with you," a man says, and I startle out of my thoughts.

When did the gate open? When did he enter?

"The Lord is with you and has greatly blessed you!"

The shuttle in my hand shakes as I point it toward the man, ready to defend myself.

There must be somewhere to hide, but the thought is barely out of my mind when peace settles in me.

“Mary, you will have a son. He will be called the Son of the Highest and the Lord will give Him the throne of His father David.”

My thoughts chase each other like a flock of young lambs. *Reign on the throne of David? Son of the Highest? You will have a son?*

“But I’m still a virgin. How can I have a baby?”

“God will implant His Spirit in you.”

In me? Who am I? Momma, where are you? I need help.

“Your Aunt Elizabeth is six months pregnant. Nothing is impossible with God.”

Nothing is impossible? Talking to an angel is impossible. Me chosen by the Almighty? That’s impossible. But here he is. And here I am. Trembling, I bow before him. “I am the Lord’s willing servant.”

As quickly as he arrived, he is gone. I try to run the shuttle through the warp threads but I can't keep the weave right. *What just happened?*

"God will implant His Spirit in you." *What will I tell Papa? And Joseph? They'll never believe me. No one will believe me.* I sink to the floor and sob. *Lord, help me. I'm alone.*

"Your Aunt Elizabeth is pregnant." *Would she believe me? Maybe?*

I walk to the cistern, splash water on my face, and take a long drink.

It's time to start dinner. Bread. I can make bread. But I drop the kneading trough.

Mamma calls at the gate. As I help her with her basket and cloak, I glance at the sun. *I have to tell her before the men get home.* "Mamma, I had a visitor while you were gone."

She flattens a lump of bread dough and slaps it on the oven. "One of the neighbors?"

"No, Mamma. An angel."

She stops and looks at me. "Now, child, angels don't just show up for regular people."

"But the people who saw angels were regular people. Jacob was running away from home. Gideon was hiding in a winepress winnowing grain. They weren't big or strong. I was weaving and he stood right there." I point to the corner where the man appeared.

"Did he have a message?"

"He said Aunt Elizabeth is six months pregnant."

"My sister, Elizabeth? At her age? That's impossible!"

"He said it's so."

"But why would the Lord send an angel to you to deliver that news?"

I catch my breath. *She doesn't believe me about the angel. She won't believe the message. What do I say?* The men come through the gate at that moment, sparing me the need to answer that question. Mamma's cousin Jacob is with them.

Papa smiles. "Look who just came back from Jerusalem."

Mamma's family are all priests, so someone is always headed to or from Jerusalem.

Mamma greets him with a kiss. "You must tell me how everyone is doing. Did you see Zechariah?"

I look at her, but she carries on as if she's just catching up with the family.

Jacob laughs. "Funny you should mention him. I'm a week late returning home because I heard rumors in Jerusalem, and I had to visit them to see if they are true. It seems the Lord has chosen to bless him in his later years. Your sister Elizabeth is with child, in her sixth month."

Mamma looks at me, eyes wide. "At her age! The Lord is gracious!"

He looks at me. "He is. But Elizabeth is having a rough time. She has requested that Mary come to help her in her final months."

Mamma shakes her head. "We are getting ready for the wedding. She doesn't have time to go down there. We'll have to figure something else out."

The evening is filled with chatter as Jacob, Mamma, and Papa catch up on the family and everything in Jerusalem.

Later, while we are cleaning the dishes, I tell Mamma, "I think I need to go visit Aunt Elizabeth. I can help her prepare for her baby."

"But we have so much to do to get ready for your wedding."

"I can do most of it there. You know she would do anything for me. Please. She needs my help."

She looks at me and sighs. "There's a division of priests gathering for Jerusalem. They'll leave in two days. You could travel with them. I'll talk to your Papa."

I throw my arms around her neck. "Oh, thank you, Mamma!" *And thank You, Lord.*

Elizabeth

I SCOOT TO THE edge of the bed and start the count. *One* – feet firmly on the floor. *Two* – deep breath, shoulders back. *Three* – pull in my stomach muscles and stand up.

Feet firm. Breathe. *If it takes me this much just to stand at six months, how will I make it to nine?*

"Leah!" No answer. Zechariah hired her a month ago to help me, but she is never around when I need her. *She needs to go back to her house.*

I grab my walking stick and start moving toward the stalls. The herdsman will be here soon for the cow and her calf. If Leah hasn't milked her, I'll need to do it.

Pain shoots through my hip with my first step. "Leah!" No answer.

Another step and more pain. "Zechariah!" *That's useless. He can't hear me.*

I limp across the courtyard, pausing every few steps. Halfway there, my hip gives out and I collapse. *Lord, how am I supposed to raise Your prophet, if I can't even carry him?*

Zechariah runs across the courtyard and kneels next to me. I lean against his shoulder. *So many things I wish I could tell you.*

The herdsman calls at the gate.

"Leah!" Still no answer.

I tap Zechariah, motioning to the cow then the gate, but he remains focused on me. I grasp his hands and point to the cow again. Reluctantly, he gets the animals, delivers them to the herdsman, then comes back and sits with me on the ground.

After a few moments he helps me to my feet, and we hobble to my stool by the oven. Once I am seated, he rubs my back. Between his gentle hands and the sun's warmth, I'm soon able to move and start the chores that should have been completed an hour earlier. Leah finally comes in, a basket of vegetables on her head.

Zechariah meets her at the gate, motioning to the stall, me, and the center of the courtyard.

She laughs. "I was just at the market."

"We've talked about this before," I interject. "You need to have the cow ready to go when the herdsman comes. You can go to the market later."

"I don't like to go to the market when it's hot. And I get the best produce first thing."

Deep breath. *Slow to anger, abounding in love. Can I be like You?* Zechariah is not so kind. He takes the basket from her arms and waves her out the gate.

"But I thought you needed help."

"I guess I don't."

Except, I do. I start to grind the grain and my back twists at the weight of the millstone. I take a sharp breath and wince.

Zechariah sits on the floor and takes the handle from me.

This won't do. He should be at the city gates where at least he can write his thoughts to the men, not stuck here doing women's work.

I try to show him that I'm okay, but he won't leave. Finally, I allow him to help me, and he settles happily beside me.

Shortly after the sixth hour, as I'm kneading bread, a man calls at the gate. I look up, sigh, and start to get up. Zechariah points questioningly at the gate and rushes to open it. My cousin Jacob stands outside. He greets us each with a kiss on the cheek. "I heard the rumors in Jerusalem and had to stop and see if they were true. The Lord has smiled on you."

Having a capable person here to help is a relief. But too soon, it's time for him to return to Galilee. As he prepares to leave, I ask a favor. "Please stop in Nazareth and ask my sister to send Mary to help me. I know she is getting ready for the wedding, but we can do most of that here. I need someone reliable."

Two weeks later, I am singing to my baby while I sift grain. I can feel him fluttering in my womb and pause to enjoy the moment I had resigned myself to never knowing. *Thank you, Lord, for Your great mercy.*

A cart clatters to a stop outside the gate and Mary bursts through. "I'm here, Auntie!"

At the sound of her voice, my baby's gentle movements turn into a sharp jump, and I know in my spirit that she carries the One my son will herald.

She is every bit the help I hoped she'd be in my remaining months. She becomes my hands and feet as I slow down and my confidant on days when I'm afraid that I'm too old to succeed in the task before me. I open my heart to her when the fears of being an unwed, pregnant woman overwhelm her. Sometimes we whisper and laugh like little girls as the difference in our ages disappears in our intertwined call.

Together, we encourage each other. "What the Lord calls you to, He will take you through." She said it first, but it soon becomes our morning and evening greeting.

When it's time for the baby to be born, she stays by my side, from sunset until mid-afternoon the following day. When he finally arrives, she takes him from the midwife and cares for him while I sleep. For the next week, he is in her arms more than mine. *Thank you, Lord, for a capable helper.*

On the eighth day, the elders and neighbors gather for the circumcision. Mary holds my hand as he cries.

The rabbi raises a cup of wine. "Our God, and the God of our fathers, raise up this child to his father and mother, and let his name be called in Israel, Zechariah, the son of Zechariah."

I jump up. "His name is John."

Rabbi looks at me. "None of your family is named John."

"That is the name the angel gave."

They motion to Zechariah. He scribbles on a writing tablet and hands it to the rabbi.

"So be it. And let his name be called in Israel, John, the son of Zechariah. Let his father rejoice in the issue of his loins, and his mother in the fruit of her womb."

Zechariah takes John in his arms and speaks for the first time in ten months. "Blessed is the Lord God of Israel, for He has visited and redeemed His people, and has raised up a horn of salvation for us in the house of His servant David."

He holds the boy close to his chest, seemingly unaware of everyone staring at him. "And you, my child, will be called the prophet of the Highest; for you will go before the face of the Lord to prepare His ways."

I wrap my arm around Mary.

She whispers to me, "Can we do this?"

I pull her head into my chest. "The Lord will take us through. Help us, Lord!"

Now hope does not
disappoint, because the love of
God has been poured out in our
hearts by the Holy Spirit who
was given to us.
Romans 5:5

Mary's Father

THE CARAVAN OF PRIESTS pulls into the village. I strain to see if my daughter is with them, but they're too far away. I catch Joseph searching the travelers, also. "Shall we start cleaning up?"

Elizabeth should have had her baby a month ago. I expected Mary to return last week.

She should be preparing for her wedding, but she asked to go help with the baby. She could ask me for a pet camel, and I'd find a way to get it for her. Our youngest of five daughters – no sons. By the Law of Moses, my name will be carried by my sons-in-law. And, by my choice, Joseph, Mary's betrothed, will inherit my masonry business.

I pick up my chisel to put it away.

"Papa! Joseph! I'm back." Mary is running down the road. She throws herself in my arms and I spin her a couple of steps before almost dropping her.

"I'm getting too old for that." I kiss her forehead. "And so are you."

She laughs then smiles shyly at Joseph. "I had so much fun with Aunt Elizabeth! Thank you for letting me go." She chatters incessantly while we clean and put away our tools.

I grasp her hand as we head home. "It has been too quiet around here with you gone."

Joseph opens the gate and I call, "Anna, I picked up a wanderer on my way home. Maybe she will liven up the house a bit."

Anna rushes across the courtyard, wiping her hands on her robe. "Mary!"

After dinner, Anna sets some roasted grain out. "How is everyone doing? How is my sister? Tell me about her baby."

Mary takes a handful of grain and picks at it, chewing it slowly. "First, I have to tell you the rest of the angel's message. I didn't tell you before because, well. . ." She picks a couple more pieces of grain from her palm and chews them.

Anna leans forward. "What is it, child?"

Joseph stands. "I'll go upstairs so you can talk about this privately."

Mary reaches up. "No! I need you to hear this. I need you to stay." She lowers her voice. "You need to know, too."

She takes a deep breath. "The other thing he said, well, he said it first." She pauses, then rushes to finish in one breath. "He said I'm going to have a son and he will be called the Son of the Highest, and that the Lord God will give Him the throne of His father David."

I slap Joseph on the back. "Well, at least we know you will have a son. Why would he tell you so far before the wedding?"

Tears fill her eyes. "No, Papa. Not after the wedding. Now. I am pregnant."

I look around the room several times before my glare lands on Joseph.

He shakes his head, jumps up, and storms out the gate.

Anna takes Mary's hands. "There must be a mistake. Sometimes we miss a cycle. It's okay."

She sobs. "No, Mamma. I know it's hard to understand. I couldn't either."

I interrupt, pointing to the door. "He does this to you and leaves you to deal with the consequences alone!"

"No, Papa, it's not like that." She throws herself on the ground at my knees. "I have not been with any man. And Joseph would never dishonor me, or you, like that. Please."

I stare at her silently. Anna cries beside her.

Mary reaches into the folds of her robe. "Aunt Elizabeth sent you a letter. Please, maybe it will help."

She hands me a letter, sealed with Zechariah's seal.

I take it without looking at my daughter. "I don't know what she can say that will make this any better."

"She wouldn't tell me what she wrote, only that I should give it to you when you couldn't believe me."

I break the seal and unroll the parchment. "Elizabeth, wife of Zechariah the priest. To my dearest sister and her husband. Grace and peace to you.

"By the time you read this letter, Mary will have told you about the message she received from the angel. I know it is difficult to believe, but you must. Please, let me tell you what happened with me.

"When Mary arrived at my home, at the sound of her voice, my babe, still in my womb, leaped. Anna, you know how babies move. This was not like that. It was as if he were trying to reach through me to touch Mary. She had told me nothing, but I knew she was also with child, and not an ordinary child, but the Holy One for Whom we have prayed.

"When the angel visited Zechariah in the Temple, he said our son would come in the spirit of Elijah, to prepare the way for the Lord's anointed One. Your daughter is blessed to bear that One. I knew that as soon as her greeting reached my ears.

"She has not done anything disgraceful. Remember the words of Isaiah, 'A virgin will conceive and bear a son and they will call him Immanuel.'[1]

"I know it is too wonderful to think that the Lord would visit your home in such a way. I felt the same way when Zechariah returned from Jerusalem. But, if the Lord can cause an old woman, who has been barren all her life, to know the joy of nursing a baby, why can He not cause a virgin to conceive?

"Before you do anything harsh or hasty, please fast and pray. Ask the Lord to reveal the truth to you. And, if you cannot bear what Mary has told you, please send her back to me. Do not cast her out alone."

"I, Zechariah, who wrote this letter for my wife, attest that every word of it is true."

I lay the letter on my lap and look at Mary. "Is that what happened?"

Tears stream down her face as she nods. "Yes, Papa. Every word of it. I swear, I would never do anything to dishonor you, or Joseph, or mother, or the Lord. I love you." She falls on her knees before me. "Please believe me. I love you."

"Either you convinced your aunt to make up an unbelievable story, or you are telling the truth."

Anna picks up the letter, as if she can decipher the words. "My sister doesn't tell stories. If she said this is how it happened, we can be sure of it."

"But it's too much. Why would the Lord choose us?"

"Papa, why does the Lord choose anyone? Why Abraham? Why Moses? I don't know why. But when He told me, I said yes. Please, Papa, help me."

I pull her into my arms. "We talk all the time about the coming of the Lord's salvation. But who thinks he would come to their home? And as a baby?"

Mary wipes her tears on my sleeve.

I whisper Isaiah's words. "By the way of the sea, beyond the Jordan, in Galilee of the Gentiles. The people who walked in darkness have seen a great light; those who dwelt in the land of the shadow of death, upon them a light has shined." [2]

"Has the Lord truly brought His light into our home? Oh, my daughter, what will we do?"

"Papa? You don't know?" She begins sobbing again.

"My precious daughter." I pull her into my lap like when she was little. "You knew what to do. You said yes. Now we put our hope in His faithfulness."

---

1. Isaiah 7:14
2. Isaiah 9:1b-2

Joseph

I BOLT THROUGH THE gate, slamming it behind me, and sprint down the street. I don't know where I'm going, but I know where I can't be.

"I'm pregnant." Mary's words tumble in my mind crushing my heart to pieces.

Then her father's look. Anger, disappointment. But it wasn't me.

I stop by the well but have nothing to draw water with. I take a breath and walk through the city gates. The gatekeeper calls, "I'll be locking the gate soon. I can't open it until morning."

"Peace to you." I shuffle toward the workshop. Since Heli apprenticed me, it's been a place of security and joy.

The door scrapes on the paving stones as I open it. We've been meaning to fix that for months, but never remember after we start our day. I grab the tools and fashion a support in the fading light. *Something I can fix.* I drop my chisel and latch the door, looking around at the tools and blocks of stone. *This used to be home. Now what?*

What do I do? If I expose Mary, she will be stoned. If I accept her, I'll never be able to trust her, and I don't want to live like that. If I don't marry her, what will become of my contract with Heli? But Mary has broken that contract. *Is this why it took her so long to answer at the betrothal ceremony? What will Mom say?*

I slide to the ground against a block and stare into the sky. *Lord, when I came here, I was sure You were guiding me, providing for me. Now, all I have is a broken heart. They say You are near to the brokenhearted. Help me know what to do.* Sobs wrack my body. *Why do you keep taking away those I love?*

When I have no more tears, I roll to my back and watch the clouds dance across the moon. *I could have danced with Mary that way. I can't let them stone her. We can quietly go to the judge. Maybe she can go live with her aunt and spare her family here the shame. What does it matter what she does?*

I finally drift off to sleep, but I don't rest. My dreams are filled with angry mobs chasing Mary. Right as they are about to throw her off a cliff, a blinding light washes out the scene. I fight to run away, but my feet won't move. The shadow of a man forms in the middle of the light, and the brightness subsides.

The man speaks. "Joseph, son of David, don't be afraid to take Mary as your wife. She has told you the truth. The child she bears is conceived by the Holy Spirit. She will give birth to a son, and you are to name him Jesus because he will save his people from their sins."

He disappears and I wake up. The first colors of dawn stretch across the sky. I pull my cloak around me and hug my knees. *Was that real or am I trying to make excuses for her? Give me a sign, Lord.*

Heli opens the door and smiles at me. "I was hoping you were here."

"I didn't know where else to go."

"I apologize for blaming you." He sits on a stone beside me and pulls a parchment from his robe. "Elizabeth sent a letter back with Mary. I'd like you to read it. You need to know that she is a daughter of Aaron and the wife of a priest. I have never known her to speak anything but the absolute truth. You can trust what you read here."

He hands me the parchment. I look at it, afraid of what I might find inside.

"You don't have to read it here. Take your time. I'll handle things today."

But I need something normal or I'll crumble like a faulty stone. I look at the scroll then Heli.

He guides me to the door. "Go."

Where do I go? I can't go home. Is it even my home anymore? I wander through the fields and find a tree to sit under. I stare at the letter a long time before I gather the courage to open it.

Elizabeth writes that she knew, at the sound of Mary's voice, that she bore the child of the Almighty. She recites the prophecies of the Holy One and promises that Mary has done no wrong.

The letter falls to the ground beside me as I remember my dream. *She has told you the truth. The child she bears is conceived by the Holy Spirit.*

The workmen in the fields call to each other. Through the city gates, I see the women gathering in the marketplace. So many people I've grown to love. *What would they do if they knew what was happening?*

And Mary. Always so generous and thoughtful. And honest. I read the letter one more time. *I don't need a sign.*

Heli puts down his chisel when I rush into the shop. "What is it, my son?"

"None of this makes sense. Why me? Why Mary?"

He shakes his head. "Jacob was a deceiver, yet through him, the Almighty chose to birth all of Israel. Who are we to question His plan?"

"I don't understand."

He pulls me into a tight embrace. "We don't have to understand. We only need to hope in Him."

We sit on the stone slab, watching people come and go from the village.

After some time, I sigh. "No one will believe us. We will be a shame to the whole family."

He pats my leg. "If, in our shame, the Almighty is honored, so be it."

So be it.

Now may the God of hope fill
you with all joy and peace in
believing, that you may abound
in hope by the power of the
Holy Spirit.
Romans 15:13

Joseph's Mother

Author's note:

Please forgive me for interrupting the story. If you have not read the Introduction yet, it is important that you do so now. It provides the necessary, historical context for this chapter.

I tilt the jug to scrape the final grains of barley. If no one else shows up, I'll have enough bread to last through Sabbath.

Sarah pours it through the millstone and begins grinding it. "Mom, why is it our job to take care of everyone?"

"It is our honor to entertain travelers. To turn away a guest would be to turn away the Lord Himself."

"Caesar made the mess by taxing everyone. He should figure out how to house them. It's not fair."

"Life isn't fair. But the Lord is always faithful."

"I still don't like it."

I pat her shoulder. "But Joseph will be home soon to register the family land. Aren't you excited to see your brother?"

"I suppose. Will Mary come with him?"

"Not until they're married. Besides, she's probably busy helping her mom. All the men with property in Nazareth have to go there to register, too."

A knock at the gate interrupts our conversation.

I sigh deeply. *Lord, can you send manna along with all these people?*

I unlatch the gate and lift it, so it doesn't scrape as I lug it open. "Sorry, the hinge is broken."

A tall, young man stands before me smiling. He's changed so much since I last saw him, but I clearly see his father in his beautiful face. I throw my arms around his neck, "Joseph!"

"Hi, Mom." He kisses my cheeks then wraps his arms around me.

I hold him for a long time and the stress of the past months melts away.

He kisses the top of my head then reaches out and ruffles Sarah's hair. "Anna sent some grain and herbs." He steps out of the gate and grabs a cart. "And I brought someone with me."

Mary follows him through the gate.

Sarah pushes past me. "Mary!"

I reach toward her. "Why did you come with him?"

Sarah grabs her hand. "Come with me. You can help me make the bread and tell me all about what's happening in Galilee!"

Mary laughs. "Nothing ever happens in Galilee."

Joseph pulls the cart into an empty animal stall. "I'm glad they get along so well."

I look at the two girls working at the millstone. "Every feast she begs to be allowed to go so she can see Mary. But why did you bring her? I'm sure her mother needs her."

He takes a deep breath. "I've been trying to decide the best way to tell you." He chews on his upper lip. "Mom, Mary is pregnant. We've already been wed and we're going to stay here."

I look across the room at Mary and force a smile. "Well, such are the passions of youth." I brush some imaginary wrinkles off my robe. "You have done the honorable thing."

Joseph interrupts. "Mom. No, it's not like that."

I hold up my hand. "Hush! We will speak no more of it. What's done is done and we will move on. Let's get you settled. There is still a little space upstairs."

As soon as Sabbath is over, Joseph is in the market with the day laborers. When he comes home that evening, before eating dinner, he asks for a lamp. Mary holds it as he repairs the gate hinge. By the time he's finished, four neighbors have asked him to make repairs on their homes.

He works just as hard as he did after his dad died, sunup to after sundown, six days a week.

A few days later, Joseph and Mary pull me aside. Joseph takes my hands. "Mamma, we need you to know about the baby." They spin a tale about an angel telling each of them that the baby would be the son of God. *You don't need to lie. One day, you'll understand the depths of a parent's love.*

But I couldn't ask for a better daughter-in-law. She knows what needs to be done and often has it completed before I think to ask. And she still blushes every time Joseph walks in the room.

For her sake, I pray everyone is done registering before the baby is due. But, as her time grows close, we see more travelers. *How many people have property in Bethlehem?*

Early one afternoon Mary is spinning wool. I notice her slowing down and rubbing her belly occasionally.

"Is it time?"

She smiles apprehensively. "Maybe?"

I look upstairs.

Sarah says what I'm thinking. "It's too crowded up there. Can she use the storage room?"

"No, all the food would become unclean."

"What about a stall? We could hang a sheet up to make a quiet room."

"That's perfect! Run get some water." I grab a broom and start sweeping.

Mary begins sobbing. "I want my mamma."

I hold her tight. "Bless you, my daughter. She would be here if she could." *Your father probably won't ever allow her to see you again.*

We finish cleaning the stall and begin preparing the evening meal for all the guests. Mary keeps working, though her pains are coming faster.

Late afternoon, a woman calls at the gate.

Mary cries out, "Aunt Elizabeth!" She hurries to the gate and pulls it open.

An older woman, with a baby on her back, wraps her in a long embrace. "Thanks be to the Lord! I'm not too late!"

Mary takes the baby off her back and smothers him with kisses. "Why are you here?"

"Your mom asked me to come be with you. She can't get away because of all the relatives coming and going."

Mary grasps her belly and takes a sharp breath. A moment later, she lets out a sigh.

Elizabeth holds her hand. "Sit down. Rest. I can help with the cooking."

Mary shakes her head. "I feel better if I'm moving. But you can still help. Sarah just finished grinding the barley. Can you make the bread?" She turns to me. "Aunt Elizabeth makes the best bread."

The older lady smiles and grabs the kneading trough.

The four of us chat as we prepare supper. Throughout the afternoon, Mary takes more frequent and longer breaks. She is leaning against the wall with her back to the gate when Joseph comes in from the fields. His eyes widen, and he looks helplessly at me. I laugh. "You get upstairs with the men. We'll take care of her."

He puts his hand on Mary's shoulder as if he expects her to crumble. She turns and embraces him.

I throw up my hands. "Okay. Stay then. But when it's time for the baby to be born, you go upstairs. This is no business for a man."

With Joseph there, Mary relaxes. They whisper and laugh together, and he holds her closely each time a wave of pains hit.

I try to keep myself busy with Elizabeth. "How many other children do you have?"

She smiles and pulls the baby close to her. "He is our only one. We had given up hope. But last year, when my husband was offering incense at the temple, an angel visited him and told him we would have a son. Here he is."

I reach out and touch the boy's head. "Really? Just like Abraham and Sarah! Do you think he might be...." I hardly dare finish. But I must know. "The Promised One?"

She laughs. "Oh, no! The angel said he's the forerunner. The Messiah is over there about to be born." She nods toward Mary. "Did they not tell you?"

"They told me, but... How?"

"I know it's hard to believe but trust me. That is not an ordinary baby."

"So, you believe their story?"

She shakes her head. "It's not a story. John recognized Him when they were both still in the womb. I knew before Mary said a word to me about it."

I look up at the sky. The first stars are beginning to appear. "I don't know."

"I understand. Ask the Lord to help you see." She hands me John and goes to check on Mary. "I think it's time to call the midwife."

Hilda comes in with her usual cheery greeting. "Well, my dear, let's have a baby!"

She takes Joseph by the arm and leads him to the stairs. "Up you go. This is women's work. We'll let you know when it's over."

He looks back at Mary. Hilda points up the stairs. He sighs and obeys.

It's not long before the baby arrives – a beautiful boy. My heart melts when I hear his first cries.

Joseph rushes down the stairs without waiting to be called. He tries to take the boy from the midwife.

She holds up her hand. "First let me get him cleaned up and swaddled. Then you can hold him."

By the time Mary has washed herself and changed her robe, the baby is ready to nurse, but Joseph sits beside them. Mary falls asleep on his shoulder.

He rests his head against the wall and also falls asleep.

I take the baby and place him in the manger, then leave the three of them to rest.

The midwife gathers her supplies. I walk with her to let her out the gate. A commotion down the way interrupts our farewells.

A group of shepherds work their way down the street, arguing. One of them sees us and rushes ahead. He grasps Hilda's shoulders then calls back to his friends, "It's the midwife! We've found Him."

She laughs, "Amos! What are you up to? You'll wake the whole town!"

"I hope so! They all need to know. The angel told us the Savior was born today and we'd find Him here, wrapped in swaddling clothes and lying in a manger." He looks at me. "Did you leave the Savior in a manger?"

"It was the only quiet place in the house, and I'd thank you to let it stay that way."

"Please, we will be quiet. Just let us see Him."

Joseph peeks his head around the curtain. "What's happening?"

"Nothing, my son. I'll send them away."

"Mom, he said an angel sent him. When will you believe? Come, see Him."

Mary sits beside the manger and picks up the baby.

The men approach them as if they are entering the Temple itself. They bow to the baby and offer prayers of thanksgiving to the Lord.

Elizabeth stands beside me. "Do you believe them, now?"

I look at the scene in front of me. Joseph, with his arm protectively holding Mary, the baby sleeping in her arms. It could happen in any home in Israel.

But the shepherds, leaving their sheep to come worship an infant at the command of an angel. And Elizabeth. And my son. *Has this ever happened in Israel?*

I look at her and smile. "I think I do."

But we know that when He is
revealed, we shall be like Him,
for we shall see Him as He is.
And everyone who has this
hope in Him purifies himself,
just as He is pure.
1 John 3:2b–3

The Shepherd

I HOLD MY SON'S hand as we finish our walk around the sheepfold. "It looks like everyone is safe for the night. You did a great job, Benjamin."

In the moonlight, I see a smile spread across his face.

We settle by the fire with my brothers, cousins, and their children. Grandpa flashes a toothless smile. "He will be ready to stay with me by harvest time."

"He might be ready but I'm not." I pause briefly. "I remember my first season alone with your dad. Those were special times. Being out here without our dads, built character."

Benjamin leans against my chest. "Papa, tell me the story of King David."

"Again? You should be able to tell me by now."

"But I like you to say it."

I ruffle his hair. "David started as a shepherd boy much like you. He spent his days in these same fields tending sheep. Here, he learned to use his sling to chase off bears and lions. He spent his days praising the Almighty. So, when the Lord was ready to anoint a new king, He looked past the mighty warriors and the strong men and He chose a boy who knew how to praise Him, someone he knew He could trust to obey."

"But he didn't always obey, did he Papa?"

"He made mistakes, as we all do. But he never made the same mistake twice. And he always repented."

My youngest cousin blurts out. "And God promised he would always have a son on the throne."

"As long as his sons obeyed. But they didn't. After King Solomon, there were many who forgot where their strength came from, so He removed that strength from them."

My littlest nephew, hiding on my brother's lap asks, "Has he forgotten us forever?"

His dad kisses his forehead. "No, my son, never forever. Even when we forget Him, He remains faithful. One day He will send a savior to free us from our enemies."

"Judas Maccabee tried that, didn't he Papa?"

"He did. But he forgot what his father had told him about always honoring the Lord. He and his sons became just as bad as the Greeks they overthrew."

"When will He come back to us?"

"I don't know, my son. But we must always live for Him and never give up hope."

I lay back in the grass and study the sky. "The One who created the stars and hung them in place is our hope."

I point out a few familiar stars, ones I consider my friends after years in the field.

A new, bright star catches my attention. "Grandpa, have you seen that star before?"

He looks where I'm pointing. "I don't think so."

We watch it while Grandpa names strange stars he remembers. "There's always the falling stars in the sixth month. The Morning Star grows bright sometimes."

It falls from its place.

"Where's it going, Papa?"

"Stars fall, sometimes. Watch it."

"It's going to hit the mountain!"

Do I tell him they always disappear first? But it doesn't. It grows brighter. "Grandpa?"

He doesn't respond.

The star continues to move closer.

"Grandpa!" I pull my eyes away from the star. He stands frozen, staring at the sky.

"Run!" I shout to the others.

The light continues to grow stronger until it's brighter than midday. I hunch protectively over Benjamin.

"Do not be afraid." The voice comes from everywhere at once.

I look over my shoulder. A man steps out of the brightness. *An angel?*

"I have wonderful news for you."

I relax my grip on Benjamin and the others slowly return.

"The savior, Christ the Lord, has been born today in the City of David."

A savior? In the city of David? Bethlehem?

"You will find the baby wrapped in swaddling clothes, lying in a manger." Suddenly, the sky fills with angels calling, "Glory to God in the highest!"

Another group shouts back, "Peace on earth, goodwill towards men."

They call back and forth to each other. Then suddenly, they are gone.

Silence settles over the countryside as one-by-one the stars reappear.

I sit on a stone, staring at the sky, and breathing deeply.

Benjamin tugs on my hand. "Papa, let's go to Bethlehem. Let's go see the baby!"

The children start running. "Let's go see the baby!"

"Wait!" Grandpa calls after them.

They keep running.

My brother grabs my arm. "Come on! Let's go!"

As we approach the city I ask, "How will we know where this baby is?"

"Papa, the Lord will show us."

Grandpa points down the street where a woman is leaving a house. "There's only one woman who would be going out this late at night."

He rushes toward her, "It's the midwife! We've found Him!"

Another woman steps up to block the gate.

Benjamin pushes forward. "Please ma'am, the angels told us a baby was born tonight and He would be the savior. May we see Him please?"

A young man steps from behind a sheet. "Mom, when will you believe? Come, see Him."

Peace like I've never known settles over me as I walk into the house. Just as the angel said, the baby is resting in a manger. His mother picks him up and motions for us to come near.

I kneel next to Benjamin. "You used to be this tiny.

"He who scattered Israel will gather him, and keep him as a shepherd *does* his flock."[1] I reach out and touch the baby's toes. *Little shepherd, are you ready to take care of your flock?*

---

1. Jeremiah 31:10

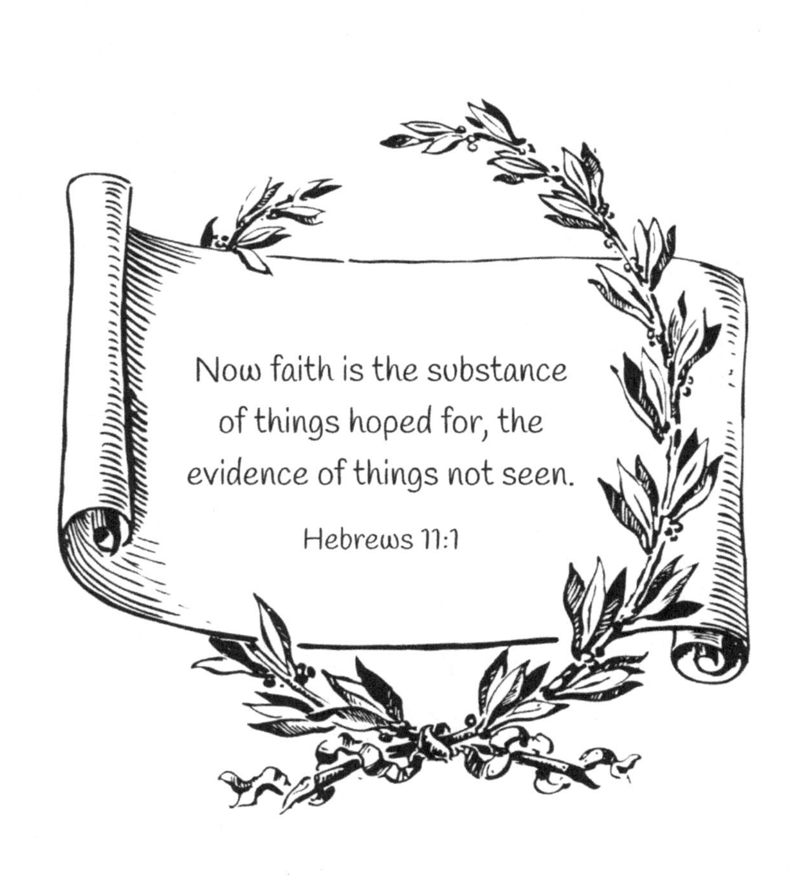
Now faith is the substance
of things hoped for, the
evidence of things not seen.
Hebrews 11:1

Simeon

I WRAP MY CLOAK tight to fight off the pre-dawn chill and watch for the sun to peek over the horizon. As its first rays light the sky, the shofar sounds, calling worshippers to the temple. I take my place at the back of the crowd with the other laymen, waiting as the priests draw lots for the morning worship duties. I can think of no better way to start my day.

After the final blessing, I remain in the courtyard enjoying the peace. Watching the priests making their sacrifices at the altar, I'm struck by the cost of that peace.

One of the scribes approaches me. "Simeon, my friend, it's good to see you."

I nod to him. "Blessings in the name of the Lord."

"Have you thought about what will become of your land once you are gathered to your fathers? You should consider leaving it to the temple."

I laugh at him. "You talked to me about it just last week. It is not my time."

"But how can you know? Many men younger than you have already left this life. It would be a shame if someone who did not care for the temple were to receive all that land."

"The Holy Spirit has shown me that I will not die before I see His Messiah. I have not seen the Messiah. Don't worry."

"After all the Romans have taken from you, do you want them to have your land, too?"

I pat him on the shoulder. "Am I your friend or do you just want my purse?"

I walk toward the southern wall, looking over the city and west toward Egypt. *He is right. I might as well donate everything to the temple.*

My eldest son died in the famine. His younger brother, Amos, joined the Roman auxiliary. He promised that he would be able to keep the Law but, as the years went on, his letters showed he didn't. Five years ago, his cohort aided with peacekeeping during the spring feasts. He visited me but refused to go to the Temple. I spoke to him more harshly than I should have, and he stormed out of the house. His years of service should be over, but I still haven't heard from him.

I pray for him every day, but I don't even know if he's still alive.

So much for a peaceful start to my day.

I shuffle down the hill and toward my olive grove alone, surrounded by the crowd.

Yet, I will hope in the Lord.

I will bless the Lord at all times; His praise shall continually be in my mouth.[1]

Do I hope? I'm sorry, Lord, I can't praise you today.

I force myself to square my shoulders and climb the Mount of Olives as one who trusts the Lord and believes in the hope of His promises. *How many hours have I spent on this mountain, tending my trees, making sure they have all they need? Who will take care of them after I'm gone?*

The workers are busy at the presses. I sit on a fallen log and watch them for some time. The Spirit tells me, "Only when the olive is bruised and crushed can it produce oil."

Crush me to pieces if that's what it takes to use me.

The peace I knew this morning returns. I stay at the presses until it's time for the evening sacrifice. As I stand in the courtyard while the priest slaughters the lamb, I cry to the Lord. *Help me to trust You always and put my hope in You. And bring Amos home.*

In the morning, after prayer, I return to the presses. A couple of soldiers stroll through the trees as I inspect the fruit. They watch while I sample the oil.

I pull the foreman aside. "Do we have anyone who might be in trouble with Rome?"

"No. I only hire people who will support the reputation of your name."

I look over at the soldiers. "Do you have any idea what they want then?"

"Would you like me to go ask?"

"No. No reason to invite trouble."

But I study them. One walks with the same gait as my wife did. I focus all my attention on him. He's too far away to see clearly but hope forces its way through the layers of pain and grief. *Could it be?*

His friend smacks him on the shoulder and pushes him in my direction. He takes a few steps and looks back. They continue together. And soon I see it is not beyond hope.

'Amos!" I run towards them and soon I am embracing my son.

He pulls away from me. "Father I'm sorry. I have sinned. Is it too late to return home?"

I throw my arms around his neck again. "It's never too late."

I turn to invite his friend to join us, but he is halfway across the hill.

We hurry home and, though it's still midmorning, I order the servants to prepare a feast.

We talk for hours. He tells me of his travels and wars he's fought and his family.

"But soldiers are forbidden to marry."

"Officially, yes. But many do and have children who travel with us. I have a son and two daughters. But, I want to raise them. . ." He pauses and looks around the courtyard. "I want to raise them right. To know and love our ways. But I. . . Can I come back?"

I grasp both of his hands. "The Lord visited Jacob when he was running away. And King David misused a woman then killed her husband to cover it up. But he repented and the Lord accepted him. He will accept you. It's never too late."

Amos walks across the courtyard. I whisper a silent prayer but am interrupted in my spirit. "It's time to go to the temple."

I glance at the sun. It's still two hours before the evening sacrifice.

Go, now.

"Amos, I must go to the temple now. If we stop by the mikvah, you can bathe and join me." I open the gate and hold out my hand. He follows silently.

At the temple, I purchase a goat for Amos' sin offering. As we follow the crowds to the inner courtyard, my attention is drawn to a young couple with an infant. They are no different than any of the other couples around. But I know.

"It's Him," I whisper.

“Who?” Amos follows me as I weave through the crowd toward the couple.

I approach the father. “May I see your son?”

He hands the child to me. It’s been a lifetime since I held one so tiny. I look into his eyes.

“Lord, now You are letting Your servant depart in peace, according to Your word.” A lump catches in my throat. “My eyes have seen Your salvation which You have prepared before the face of all peoples, a light to bring revelation to the Gentiles, and the glory of Your people Israel.”[2]

My son and the Messiah in one day. You are too good to me.

---

1. Psalm 34:1

2. From Luke 2:28-32

Anna

63 BC

I stand on the street with the rest of Jerusalem. The summer sun warms the morning air. Above us, the battering ram strikes the temple walls.

Bam!

I know it's coming, but I still catch my breath.

Bam!

Do they know it's a fast day and our men haven't eaten?

Bam!

In between strikes, I hear the priest singing their morning songs.

Bam!

The smoke from the altar rises in the air.

Bam!

Johanan and his dad are behind those walls.

Bam!

Salome hugs my legs.

Bam!

"Mommy, are they trying to hurt Daddy?"

Bam!

What do I say?

Bam!

This is all the Pharisees' fault.

Bam!

Rocks fall to the valley below the temple wall.

Bam!

The Romans cheer each other on.

Bam!

My heart shatters as the wall crumbles.

Stories of unmentionable horrors trickle into the city. I leave Salome with a neighbor and make my way up the hill with those returning from the valley. The unending line of biers being carried out to the mass grave hint at the truth of the tales. I search the faces on each one. *Do I hope to see them? Or not?* They tell me not one of the twelve thousand men survived, so I know....

The stench hits me well before I reach the gates. *Has anything like this ever been known in Israel?* When I step into the temple, I collapse. Destruction covers the House of Peace.

Miriam, the wife of one of the Pharisees kneels next to me.

I turn away. "Leave us alone. You called Pompey here. This is all your fault!"

She touches my shoulder and answers quietly. "Aristobulus sent envoys to Pompey, too. The Romans pitted us against each other, Pharisees against the Sadducees, Hyrcanus against Aristobulus. They've won. We all have lost. The only way we can rebuild is together."

Miriam takes me to the place where Johanan and his dad fell. Together, beside the altar. She says his dad had a sheep in his arms, and Johanan a sword, defending them both. All that's left is their blood stains.

I sit on the ground and stare at the destruction around me. *I am alone. No husband. No brother. Salome and me. What will I do?*

"I am with you. You will tell of My Hope."

I jump up and look around.

Miriam is scrubbing the stones of the altar. She puts down her rag and comes to me. "What is it, my dear?"

"Who said that?" I scan everyone working.

"Who said what?" She looks around, too. "No one said anything."

"I heard someone say, 'I am with you.'"

Miriam takes my hands. "Could it have been the Lord?"

I pull away. "The Lord hasn't spoken to us since Moses. There's no such thing as angels or spirits. Leave me alone!"

Miriam puts her arm around me. "I know that's what you've been taught, but if our only hope is for this life, is it really hope?" She embraces, then returns to her work.

I hear the voice again. "I am with you. You will tell of My Hope."

Almost 60 Years Later

The temple clears out as everyone rushes to be home before sunset. I should be at my grandson Micah's house, but the fragrance of the sacrifices and the peace in the courtyard tug at me. I sit by the wall and close my eyes.

"Granny." Thaddeus stands in front of me. "Uncle Micah sent me to get you. It's almost time to light the candle."

I take his arm, and he leads me toward Micah's house.

"How are my great-great-grandchildren?"

"They are growing strong, by the Grace of the Lord. I plan to bring Seth with me for Passover so you can meet him."

The family crowds inside the upper room. Tables, laden with the feast, line the walls.

I hug Salome. "Look at how the Lord has blessed your family."

As the sun sets, Micah's wife lights the candle. Micah leads the family in the prayers of dedication.

The little one climbs on my lap. "Did you know Judah Maccabee, Granny?"

"No, Enoch. I'm not quite old enough to remember the war with the Greeks. I did meet Hyrcanus once, after the Romans took Jerusalem."

"We need to finish that war."

I look up to see who said that. "Thadeus, Thadeus, who put such ideas into your mind?"

"It's true, Granny. The Romans don't belong here."

"My son, I have seen too many battles in Jerusalem. Our only hope is preparing our hearts for the redeemer."

He stands. "To free us from the Romans."

"To free us from ourselves."

Micah interrupts. "Granny's right. We must purify ourselves and live holy lives. We Pharisees dedicate all we have to the Lord. Every breath is spent honoring and obeying Him."

Thadeus scoffs. "Like when He says, 'Honor your father and mother?' How do you obey that command while you let Granny sleep on the streets?"

"Are you accusing me of wrongdoing? How dare you!" He leans into Thadeus' face. "I have devoted everything to the Lord. Including that which I would have given to Granny and mother. Do you think I like to see her on the street?"

"I'm right here. I can defend myself. Thadeus, it is not your place to correct your uncle. I like staying at the Temple, right there in The Presence. There's nothing like it."

"I can't stand how he pretends to be so perfect, but his own son hates him."

Micah turns away. "My son is dead. You will not speak of him again."

"Jonah is not dead. He just couldn't stand living with you. And you're too proud to admit there might be something wrong in your family."

"Both of you, sit down." I don't have to raise my voice. "Thadeus. That's enough."

"Yes, Granny."

"This is a time of rejoicing. Why are we celebrating?"

Enoch wiggles on my lap. "I know. We celebrate the Feast of Ded'cation to a'member the time they cleaned the temple after Ant'ocus Pifny filed it."

"Very good. And why did the Lord let the Greeks defile the Temple and take Jerusalem?"

"A'cause they didn't obey and trust the Lord."

"Exactly. But did the Lord stay mad at us?"

"No. He sent Judah Maccabee to get rid of the Greeks."

"That's right. He is always gracious." I kiss his cheek. "Micah, our people have spent more time rebelling against the Lord than obeying Him, but when we repent, He always forgives. The Lord does not give up on us. Don't give up on Jonah." *Please, Lord, don't give up on him. Bring him home.*

"But, Granny..."

"No, my son. Hear me. I remember when the Pharisees were a new group. They honored the Lord and they just wanted everyone to serve Him. It was good. But now, you have added so many rules that it's become a burden. The covenant of faith was made with Abraham long before the Law was given. The Lord wants our hearts. Not more rules."

"But..."

I hold up my hand. "Listen to the prophets. It's about our hearts."

The crowds jostle and push to exchange their coins and purchase sacrifices. The endless stream files through the Nicanor gate to the priests, where the stench of the slaughtered animals blends with the aroma of the meat roasted on the altar.

The men sit under Solomon's Porch arguing about the Law and Prophets and politics. And I sit at my spot near the wall, waiting. Not for anything in particular. Just waiting and praying like I often do.

Micah makes his way through the courtyard. He weaves in and out of the crowd searching for someone then starts in my direction. I look around to see who he might have seen. Then, he's next to me.

"Hi, Granny." My dignified Pharisee sits on the ground. "I need to talk to you."

"What is it, my son?"

"I've been thinking about what Thadeus said. He's right."

"Hopefully not the part about fighting against the Romans."

"No. The part about Jonah. I was always pushing him to be perfect. But not because I wanted him to honor the Lord." He gestures around the courtyard. "I was afraid of what they would say. It's always about how I look."

"So, what now?"

"That's what I want to know. What do I do now?"

"You repent, rededicate yourself to the Lord, and let Him guide you."

"But how do I bring my son home?" He pounds the ground. "I don't even know where he is!"

"No, we don't. But the Lord does. We will pray that he returns safely."

"That's not enough. What can I *do*?"

"My son, you can't fix this any more than you can fix a smashed jug. But the Lord can form His pottery however He pleases."

"I don't like it."

"None of us do. That's why we reach for the Lord in our own way. Our ancestors needed something to look at, so they ran after idols. The scribes search and study so they can know. The Sadducees try to do it through politics. And the Pharisees work to prove to the Lord how holy they are. But none of it is enough."

He leans his head against the wall. "What does He want?"

"What do the prophets say?"

He looks at me as if I've sent him back to a tutor. "Turn from your wicked ways. Quit following idols. Obey the commands."

"What else? What about 'Hear, O Israel, the Lord our God, the Lord is One!'"

"'You shall love the Lord your God with all your heart, with all your soul, and with all your strength.'"[1]

"Exactly. We are to love Him with everything we are, with a love that causes us to want to serve Him."

"That's hard, Granny. I can't do anything for Jonah?"

"We pray for him and trust the Lord to call him back."

We sit quietly for a while watching the bustle in the outer court. My attention is drawn to a young couple standing in line to purchase a dove. When they turn around, I see the man is holding a baby.

"Help me up." I lean on Micah's shoulder before he has a chance to move. "Come with me. I want to show you something. Someone."

By the time my legs decide to cooperate, the prophet Simeon has the baby in his arms. "That's who I've been talking about."

"Simeon?"

"No, the baby. The Redeemer."

Simeon looks at the mother. "A sword will pierce through your soul also. And through Him, the thoughts of many hearts will be revealed."[2]

Micah whispers. "He's full of good news."

"Have you not read the scriptures? Redemption is costly. The Messiah must suffer. And this poor young woman will have to watch it. But the Lord will carry her." *Redeem us quickly, Lord, and cut short the suffering of Your people.*

---

1. From Deuteronomy 6:4-5

2. From Luke 2:28-32

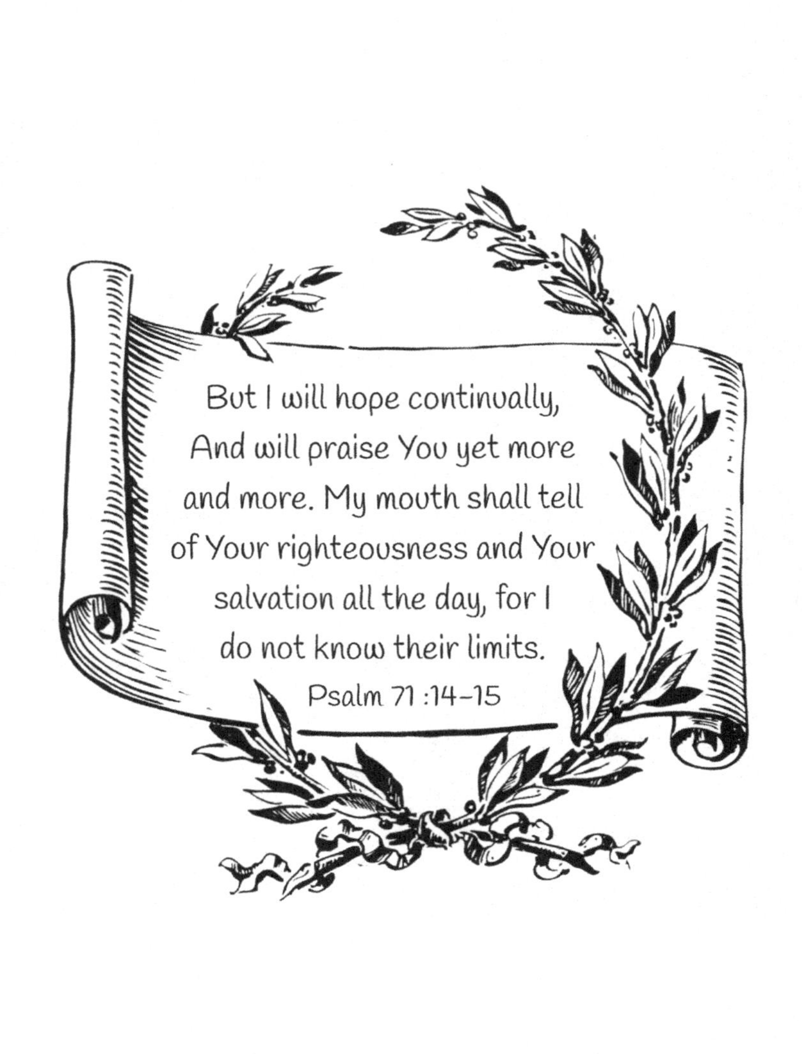
But I will hope continually,
And will praise You yet more
and more. My mouth shall tell
of Your righteousness and Your
salvation all the day, for I
do not know their limits.
Psalm 71 :14-15

The Wise Man

I CLIMB THE STAIRS and nod at my brother as I flop on my rooftop couch.

A servant hands me a drink.

Joab sits on his couch. "Long day?"

"Two men came to me disputing about a lamb. Both claimed they owned it, and both had witnesses."

"How did you decide?"

I take a drink before answering. "Remember when the two women went to King Solomon fighting over a baby? I did the same thing as Solomon. The true shepherd was immediately apparent."

"You have been blessed with the wisdom of our ancestors."

"Yes, well, there also was a widow who couldn't pay. . ."

"Do you see what I see?"

I glance at the sky where he's pointing. "What?"

"There's a new star on the Lion!"

"We aren't due for any wandering stars." I study the constellation. Sitting on the Lion's head, like a crown, is a new star.

Joab whispers, "I see Him, but not now; I behold Him, but not near; A Star shall come out of Jacob; A Scepter shall rise out of Israel."[1]

"But we're the descendants of David. I am supposed to take the throne. If not me, then my son, or his son."

"Where did you hear that?"

I run my finger around the rim of my cup. "I don't know. I guess I always knew it. Isn't that why we have continued as governors after Nebuchadnezzar brought us here?"

"Neither Father nor Grandfather ever said anything like that."

"Well, they should have. Maybe we are wrong. Maybe it is a wanderer." I start downstairs.

"It's not a wanderer." But he follows me to the library.

By the time we get there, our cousin Nathan is already searching the records.

I pull a clay tablet from the stack. "It has to be a wanderer."

Nathan doesn't look up. "Sitting on the head of the Lion? I've never heard of such a thing." He puts his tablet aside and grabs another.

I pick up a writing tablet and begin calculations. "It has to be. And we aren't leaving until we find it."

The next night, the star is there again, mocking me.

Joab stands by the balustrade, watching the kingly Lion. "It's a new star. A king has been born in Judah." He turns to look at me. "We're going to Jerusalem."

"I'm not."

"Maybe you'd find. . ."

I slam my fist on the railing. "I didn't lose anything in Jerusalem. I don't need to go find it."

Over the next months, Joab and Nathan incessantly speak of the trip and the new king. And they're constantly gathering supplies. I spend a lot of time in my private chambers.

A week before they are to leave, Joab corners me. "You need to go with us."

"I am the one who determines what needs to happen."

He grabs my shoulders. "All my life I've watched you serve our people with grace and love. But these past months, you have been angry and bitter. I miss my confident and compassionate brother."

"Of course I'm angry. Every night, that star reminds me that I'm not good enough. The Lord chose another king. What did I do wrong? What does He want from me? What am I missing?"

"Join us. I think you'll find out."

I sigh. "It can't be worse than this."

The next night, the star is not in the sky.

Four miserable months later, we arrive at King Herod's palace in Jerusalem.

Joab bows to him. "The stars told us that a great king was born here. We have come to worship him."

Herod's face clouds, but he composes himself. "We have had no children born in the palace recently. But I will have my sages look into the matter and tell you where you can find this child."

He invites us to his banquet hall. While everyone else is distracted by the musicians and dancers, he leans over to me. "Tell me about this star."

"It was a new star, crowning the Lion. None of our records show it."

"And when did it appear?"

He peppers me with questions concerning the star and the prophecies.

Finally, a messenger saves me from the interrogation. "They have discovered where the child was born."

Herod claps once. Everyone quiets and two men approach us. The older one bows. "Your majesty, we have the answer to our guests' question." He steps aside and pushes the younger forward.

After some prompting, the young man closes his eyes and recites with a quavering voice, "But you, Bethlehem Ephrathah, though you are little among the thousands of Judah, yet out of you shall come forth to Me the One to be Ruler in Israel."[2]

Herod stands. "If you leave now, you can reach Bethlehem by nightfall. When you find this king, come back and tell me where he is so I may, too, honor him."

Joab bows. "You are welcome to join us now."

"Thank you for your gracious offer. You go ahead. I must prepare my gifts for such a great king."

Nathan pushes his horse ahead of the caravan.

I call after him. "What's your hurry? We don't even know where to find this child."

"In Bethlehem. Didn't you hear the scribe?"

"I would imagine there is more than one child in Bethlehem."

"If the Lord has sent us this far, He will guide us to His king."

As he motions toward the horizon, the star reappears.

I stop my horse and watch it shoot across the sky. Then it changes course and starts falling toward us.

Joab jumps from his horse and ducks behind a bolder. Nathan and I are right behind him. The men look around confused, weapons at the ready.

The star slows and moves along the road in front of the caravan.

The three of us creep from behind the rock. Joab points and tells the captain. "Follow that star."

When we reach Bethlehem, we leave the soldiers and servants to set up camp outside the walls. The star leads us through town and floats above a small home.

Joab knocks on the gate and a young woman opens it. A small boy peeks around her robes.

"Good evening, we've come to honor the new king."

She motions for us to come in.

She scoops up the toddler and places him on her hip. "I am Mary and this is Jesus. It has been some time since anyone has referred to him as anything but a normal boy."

None of us move.

"Did you expect him to be wearing a crown and dressed in finery?" She smiles kindly.

What did I expect? Just a common home in a common town. No, not a common town. King David's town. *Of course, the king must come from here.*

Joab rushes to the cart and pulls out the chest of gold coins. "A small token of our worship."

The gate opens behind us. A muscular, tanned man enters. The woman smiles and reaches toward him. "My husband, Joseph. These men saw a star telling them a king was born."

Joseph offers us a kiss of greeting and invites us to sit while Mary finishes supper.

Nathan leans against the wall. "Your wife said it's been a long time since anyone spoke of Jesus as special. There were others before us?"

The little boy runs over to us and Joseph snatches him, planting a kiss on his nose. "Before his birth, an angel told me that he will save his people from their sins. We were living up north at the time, but I had to come home to register for the tax. I brought Mary with me, not even considering the prophecy that said the savior would be born here. Then, the night he was born some shepherds came from the field. They said the angels had told them they would find the savior here."

"Angels and shepherds?" I look at the little boy playing with his father's beard.

"And prophets. My wife's uncle, a priest, prophesied over him before he was born. And when we took him to the Temple to be dedicated, a prophet there spoke of his future."

"But why Bethlehem? We have remained faithful to him in Parthia."

"Does it matter why? The Lord declared Bethlehem. Here we are."

Here we are. But why?

Mary spreads a cloth on the ground in front of us and places a plate of bread and a dish of stew on it.

An elderly lady calls at the gate and then opens it. She hands a bowl to Mary, staring at us the whole time. "I brought some grapes for your guests."

As she leaves, another comes in. "I brought some barley stew."

Five more came after her, each bringing food.

Mary looks helplessly at Joseph who smiles. "The Lord is using their curiosity to give us a worthy feast for our guests."

After she returns to the fire, he says, "'A sword will pierce your soul, too.' That's what the prophet in Jerusalem said to Mary. I love this little boy and will do all I can to protect him. But to know that, because of his birth, my wife. . ." He ruffles Jesus' hair and hands him a piece of bread. "And this one is 'a sign that will be spoken against.' Sometimes, I think I'd rather be a tax collector than carry this burden. But the Lord, in His wisdom, chose me. So, I trust Him."

Could I obey like that?

Jesus toddles over to me and gives me the bread. I smile and thank him.

He's so little, so innocent.

I look at the humble spread before me and the bread in my hand. *Have I ever trusted the Lord like this man?*

I take a bite of the bread and study the scene around me. A simple man with more wisdom than all my council. A humble home with more to give than the riches of all of Parthia.

I see Your wisdom. Help me to trust You as he does.

---

1. Numbers 24:17
2. Micah 5:2

The Scribe

I CALL AT MY sister's gate, then open it without waiting for a reply. Abi and another young woman sit carding wool.

My nephews rush toward me. Another little boy toddles after them and then turns back to his mom.

I scoop up the youngest, Ira, swing him to my shoulders, and grab Tobiah's hand. "Sorry. I didn't know you had company."

"Come on in. Do you remember Joseph? He went to live with his uncle in Nazareth about ten years ago. This is his wife, Mary. And their son, Jesus."

"Good to meet you. How is Joseph?"

We chat for a few minutes, catching up on the happenings of Bethlehem. I set Ira down. "I need to get home. I scratched some thoughts about Jeremiah's prophecies on the wall and need to look at them."

"Mom hated when you did that."

"But she never washed them off. And there always was a perfectly charred stick near the fire."

Tobiah tugs at my robe. "Uncle Joel, listen!" He stands tall and straightens his robe. "'But you, Bethlehem Ephrathah, though you are little among the thousands of Judah, yet out of you shall come forth to me the one to be ruler in Israel, whose goings forth are from of old, from everlasting.'"[1]

"Are you sure you're only five years old? Did you grow up while I was in Jerusalem?"

"I am five." He holds up five fingers. "And Daddy says if I keep learning, I can be a scribe like you."

I kneel and put my arm around him. "Next time I visit, I will bring you a writing tablet so you can start practicing."

Ira grasps my beard and turns my head toward him. "Hee Isel. Lod one."

Abi laughs. "That's right. 'Hear, Oh Israel, the Lord your God, the Lord is one.'"

"You are a genius!" I kiss his chubby cheeks.

"Sorry it's such a short visit. I need to find the right scratches and head back to Jerusalem in the morning. Next time I'll bring the family and stay longer."

On the way back home the next morning, my mind wanders to the prophecy Tobiah quoted. "Oh Bethlehem Ephrathah." Every young boy in Bethlehem memorizes it. The thrill of that prophecy ignited my desire to become a scribe. "Out of you shall come forth to me the one to be ruler in Israel." *How long, Lord?*

A caravan clogs the city gate. It takes me a moment to decipher their language. *Parthian! I haven't been able to practice that in months.* I find a guard at the back of the group. "What took you to Jerusalem?" *That's the wrong word.* "Brings. What brings you to Jerusalem?"

"You speak Parthian. You must be a scholar." I don't understand his next sentence. He kindly repeats it in Aramaic. "We've come to greet the great king."

The great insane king. Some thoughts must never be uttered. I look up the hill to the temple. Though still under construction, travelers from around the world come to see its splendor. *How does the same man create such beauty, yet kill a high priest and even his own wife and sons out of jealousy?*

I sit at my desk in the temple workshop and read the section I wrote before I left, then continue copying.

"Behold, the days are coming," says the Lord, "That I will raise to David a Branch of righteousness; a King shall reign and prosper, and execute judgment and righteousness in the earth. In His days Judah will be saved, and Israel will dwell safely; now this is His name by which He will be called: THE LORD OUR RIGHTEOUSNESS.[2]

Come quickly, to free us.

One of the priest's sons enters the room. "King Herod wants to know where the Messiah will be born."

A couple of the other scribes look up from their work. Most continue copying without pause.

I wish he wouldn't pretend to love our traditions. "Micah said Bethlehem of Judea. My five-year-old nephew knows that." I dip my pen in the ink and continue copying.

The high priest comes to the door. "Joel, follow me."

Taking a moment to put my equipment away, I go with him. He leads me to the palace banquet hall where the Parthians sit with the king.

The priest bows and then turns to me. "These men have come from Parthia to honor the great king who was born to rule the Jews."

That great king. He was born? Herod stares at me. *That's why he wanted to know. What have I done?*

"I understand you know where he might be found."

I can't tell him. He'll slaughter the whole town. If I don't tell, he'll kill me.

"Our guests are waiting for your reply."

I was just there. If I had known, I would have searched for him myself.

Herod rises and motions to a guard.

I swallow hard. "'But you, Bethlehem Ephrathah, though you are little among the thousands of Judah, yet out of you shall come forth to me the one," My voice cracks. "The one to be ruler in Israel.'"

Lord, forgive me for betraying your anointed one. Save him. Save my family. Save my town.

Herod nods at the Parthians. "My guards will escort you to the city gates and point you on your way. If you leave now, you can reach Bethlehem by nightfall. When you find this king, come back and tell me where he is so I may, too, honor him."

As soon as the doors close behind the guests, Herod stands. "I am the king of the Jews. There will be no more talk of another king and none of you are to leave Jerusalem."

I rush home and craft a note to my brother-in-law. "You must get your family out of Bethlehem immediately."

When my daughter Lydia hears I'm going to the marketplace, she begs to go with me. She chatters all the way there. I answer with an occasional grunt.

"Did you tell Grandma that I'm learning to make bread? Mama says I can start carding wool after the next sheep shearing. Will Grandpa let me watch them shear the sheep? How is baby Ira?"

"Papa! You're not listening to me."

"I'm sorry, what my precious?"

"I asked how Baby Ira is doing and you said, 'Messiah.' Is Baby Ira the Messiah?"

"I'm sorry. I'm thinking about some of the things I wrote today."

The market is buzzing with talk of the Parthians and guesses about what Herod will do. I deliver the note to a young man with a few extra coins to encourage haste, then return home before anyone sees me.

While Lydia and my wife make supper, I sit on the floor with Jonathan, scratching letters in the dirt.

Dinah hands me the sleeping baby. "He's only five. Don't push him."

"He's doing a beautiful job."

A pounding on the gate startles the baby and she starts crying.

"Open up now, by order of King Herod."

I give the baby to Dinah and motion for them to go to the storeroom.

"Open now or I will break the door down."

"Go now." I push Jonathan toward his mom and go to open the gate.

My messenger stands, surrounded by soldiers, head down, hands tied behind him. One of the soldiers thrusts the open note into my chest. "You are guilty of treason. Come with me."

Dinah screams and rushes into the courtyard.

I say nothing as the soldier drags me from the house.

In the fortress, they tie us down and the soldiers take turns with the whip. The lashes on my back don't cut as deep as my guilt when I hear the young man's screams. *Why did I bring an innocent boy into this?*

That night, in the inner prison, I apologize a thousand times. *I'm a fool to think I could defy Herod.* The next morning, they take the boy to be crucified. His empty chains haunt me. *Herod is saving me for something. Why was I not hung beside him? Did he die quickly or is he still suffering on the cross? How many prophets sat in prison because they foretold Your messiah? He is here and I betrayed him.*

They leave me, isolated, for three days. On the fourth day, I'm dragged to the palace. Herod paces in front of his throne. "What do you know about this new king?"

I throw myself on the floor in front of him. "Only what I have already told you. The prophet Micah said he would be born in Bethlehem."

"What do you know about the Parthians?"

"I know nothing about them, oh king."

A soldier strikes my cheek. "That is a lie. You were seen talking to them when they entered Jerusalem. What do you know about them?"

"Please, I know nothing. I had been to visit my family, and we entered at the same time. We shared a polite exchange. That is all I know."

"What did they tell you?"

"Only that they are from Parthia and came to visit the great King. I thought they meant you."

Herod turns to his guard. "Gather a troop and go to Bethlehem. Kill all the baby boys two years old and younger. I will not have a rival."

A scream escapes from the pit of my belly. "Ira!"

The king turns to me. "What do you know?"

I try to stand. "Please! I know nothing."

"But you know someone. Is he the king?"

"No! He's just a baby boy."

"And baby boys grow up to lead rebellions."

Now I've killed my own nephew.

He motions to his guard. "Go."

I watch helplessly as the man marches out to destroy my family.

---

1. Micah 5:2
2. Jeremiah 23:5-6

The Soldier

Content Warning:

This story contains intense scenes that may not be appropriate for young or sensitive audiences.

Augie scampers across the courtyard, chasing the sheep-bladder ball. He grabs it and runs back toward me.

"No. Throw it."

I take his hands and the ball in mine and help him throw the ball. He squeals as it hits the dog who looks at us with annoyance.

"Go get it and throw it back to me." Augie toddles toward the dog, plops down next to him, and puts his head on the dog's belly.

"It's a good thing he's a gentle dog," my wife says as she slaps a loaf of bread on the oven.

There's a knock at the gate. The dog jumps up, tumbling Augie to the floor. One of my fellow soldiers calls, "We are to be ready to march in 30 minutes. There's an insurrection in Bethlehem."

"I'll be ready," I respond.

My wife sighs. “What is it with these Jews and their insurrections? If it’s not that, it's a festival where the whole country has to show up.”

I kiss her on the cheek. “Bethlehem doesn’t have 300 men. It can’t be much of an insurrection. I’ll be home by tomorrow evening. Now, put some food in a purse for me while I go get my uniform.”

Fifteen minutes later, I’m latching the gate and on my way. A man steps out of the shadows, and I reach for my dagger.

“Good evening, Augustus.”

In the fading light, I recognize my friend’s father.

I put the dagger back in its sheath. “Hello, Simeon. You should not sneak up on a soldier like that. It could be costly.”

“The journey you are about to take will be costly. You will leave your heart in Bethlehem.”

“What are you saying? What do you know?”

“I say only what the Spirit of the Lord tells me to say. I know only what He reveals. When you return, I will be ready to listen.”

I clap him on the back. “I’ve fought more battles than I can count. There’s nothing in a backcountry village that will hurt me.”

He nods. “I will be here when you return.”

Clouds cover the moon as we approach Bethlehem. I see no torches or other signs of an uprising that I expected. Instead, the entire city seems to be asleep. I look around at my fellow soldiers. They are scanning the hills and fields looking for the rebels.

Our centurion calls for a halt. “Set up camp in front of the city gates. Monitor the caves in the hills. No one is to leave. I will tell you the details in the morning.”

The peace of the sleepy town settles on our camp. Rather than the normal shouts, we whisper to each other, hardly daring to breathe.

I am selected for the first watch. As I position myself on the camp's perimeter, the centurion repeats, "No one leaves."

They must have someone hiding in there. Hope he gives up without a fight.

We pass the night without incident and gather at dawn for our instructions.

The centurion paces in front of us for some time before he speaks. "Men, you have sworn to protect the empire. We work as a unit and we follow instructions. We do not question. We obey.

"Jewish prophecies have predicted a king will come to set them free. We recently had visitors from Parthia who saw signs in the stars telling them a baby was born to fulfill those prophecies. King Herod wants the boy dead before he can become a threat. Since our foreign guests did not return as directed to tell us where the child is," he stops and looks towards the mountains then continues. "Men, we are soldiers. Our orders are to kill all baby boys under the age of two."

Murmurs ripple through the ranks. Seasoned soldiers drop their shields.

The centurion snaps. "Attention! We obey orders. We do not question. We defend the empire. You will pair up and go to every home in this town and its villages. Every boy two years old or younger is to be found and killed. There are no exceptions. If one of our ranks does not obey, he is an insurrectionist and will be immediately executed."

My mind races back to little Augie with his head on the dog's belly. *They're just like my baby. I can't.* I pull my sword from its sheath and drop it on the ground.

I feel the tip of a spear on my back. "It's a couple of Jewish boys. It's not worth losing your life over. I'm sure Augie wants his father," Marcus says.

I bend over and retrieve my sword.

"Good choice. Come with me."

As one unit, we storm into the city. Marcus slams his fist against a gate. "Open up, now, by order of King Herod! "

A man cracks the door open. Behind him, a boy of about five stacks firewood in the corner, and a woman sits by the fire nursing a baby.

Marcus pushes the door open and draws his sword "By order of King Herod, all baby boys are to die."

The woman screams and backs against the wall, clutching the baby to her chest. The young boy grasps her legs.

The man tries to shut the door. "No! No! You can't! Abi, run!"

I stand frozen as Marcus pushes through the gate. The father races across the courtyard, grabs his baby, and sprints toward the ladder leading to the roof.

Marcus strides toward him and thrusts his sword through father and baby. He yanks out his sword and steps back as their bodies fall to the ground.

I should have run when I could.

The woman lets out a wail. "Ira! Peter!"

"It didn't have to be both of them, but your husband decided to defy Rome." Marcus slams my shoulder as he walks by. "Let's go."

The next three homes have no young children, the fourth has a baby girl. And it's over. We file silently out of the city. Scanning the faces of my fellow soldiers, I can tell the ones who found the boys.

An old man spits on us from a rooftop. "Do you think you can defy the Almighty? People have been trying to destroy us from the beginning, but the Lord is faithful. His Redeemer will rise and you will fall!"

Marcus and a few others draw their swords. The centurion shakes his head. "We've done what we were commanded. We are finished."

I sit in my courtyard, sobbing. I want to hold Augie, but he keeps squirming away. Simeon sits beside me without saying a word.

After some time, I'm able to talk. "We killed your king."

Simeon offers a sad smile. "No, you killed innocent babies. But not our messiah."

"You weren't there. There is no way any baby survived."

"We call Him Lord and Almighty for a reason. His plans cannot be stopped, and He is Commander of all. The Messiah survived. I saw him with my own eyes yesterday."

I take a breath and stare at the old man. "How?"

"The less you know the better, my friend, but they were here and now they're gone. The Hope of Israel lives."

I look at Augie and my wife. I think of the little widow I left in Bethlehem. *How do they speak of hope? How can their hope survive?*

Joseph, Part 2

I FOLLOW MARY AND Mom, dragging the cart over the paving stones. Its clatter echoes in the silent street.

Mary stops in front of a large house. Mom sits on the cart's edge, pulling the blankets back to check on Jesus.

I whisper. "Are you sure this is the right place?"

"This is the one." Mary knocks firmly on the door.

An old man responds sleepily, "Who's there?"

"Uncle Zechariah, it's me, Mary."

There's fumbling and bumping inside and finally, the gate swings open. "Mary! What are you doing here?"

"Quiet." I put my hand on his arm and whisper. "Please, let us in and we will tell you everything."

"Joseph, Anna! Come in."

I step aside to let the women in, searching the shadows down the street before bolting the door.

Elizabeth shuffles over and wraps Mary in a hug. "What brings you here in the middle of the night? You must be exhausted."

Jesus fusses. I pick him up. "About midnight, an angel told me to take my family to Egypt because Herod is trying to kill him. We were out of the house within the hour."

Mary sobs. "I'm so scared, Auntie. I can't do this."

"Oh, my dear girl. We always knew it would be hard. But remember, what the Lord calls you to, He will take you through."

"I can't."

"You're safe here. Go upstairs and rest. You'll feel better after you sleep."

"But we need to get to Egypt."

Zechariah ushers us toward the stairs. "My girl, you need to rest, and you can't travel to Egypt by yourself. Tomorrow, we will go to Jerusalem. Someone will be headed south from there."

Elizabeth reaches for Jesus. "Leave him with me. He and John can play together until you wake up."

I pull away and put my hand protectively over his head.

"My son. Trust the Lord. He will guard you and grant you perfect peace." She takes Jesus from my arms. "Get rest. You have a long journey."

That afternoon, Zechariah recounts the stories I've known since childhood. Noah, Abraham, Joseph, Joshua, David, Jeremiah. "Our people have a heritage of hope. Trust the Lord who is Faithful."

Early the following day, we leave for Jerusalem, but Zechariah stops at the Mount of Olives. "The man we need to talk to will be here soon."

A short while later, the prophet from the temple and another man round the hill. I jump up. "Simeon!"

Zechariah laughs. "You know him?"

"He's the one who prophesied over Jesus when we came to dedicate him." I eye the man beside Simeon and step between him and Jesus. "You stand like a soldier."

"This is my son, Amos. He joined the army when he was young. But the Lord has been gracious to me and brought him home, heart and body. He was in the temple with me when you dedicated Jesus. Remember?"

I shake my head.

"What brings you to my garden?"

Has his heart truly returned home?

Amos claps Simeon on the back. "I'll go check with the foreman while you talk."

Jesus hands me a stick. I pick him up while watching Amos stride toward the foreman. *How will I ever know who to trust?*

I tell Simeon my dream.

"Oh no." He sits on a log and puts his face in his hands.

"What's wrong?"

He sighs deeply. "The Lord sent me to speak to a soldier last night – one of Amos' friends. His century was headed to Bethlehem. The Lord showed me that he would leave his heart there."

My mom gasps.

Mary grabs her hand, "I hope Abi is okay."

Simeon stands. "Let's get you to my house, then off to Egypt."

His house is busy with Amos' family and all the servants going in and out. I sit next to Zechariah in the corner. "What if one of them betrays us?"

"My son, to most of these people, you are just another traveler who Simeon has welcomed into his home. They don't know there's anything to betray."

"But Amos..."

"But Amos. We would be a sorry people if the Lord treated us as our sins deserved. Moses and David both killed men. Yet, when the Lord changed their hearts, they became our greatest leaders. Do you trust the Lord's ability to change hearts?"

Can I? Sigh.

Simeon strides through the courtyard. "I found a trader traveling to Arabia."

"Arabia? The angel told me to go to Egypt."

"He will take you to Gaza. From there, you can find a caravan going west."

I lean my head against the wall. "How am I supposed to do that? The farthest I've ever traveled is to Nazareth. What if we meet thieves or there's a storm?"

Zecheriah puts his hand on my arm. "What if the Lord proves Himself faithful? He led Moses in the same wilderness. He can lead you."

I bite my lip and blink back tears. *Why did You choose me?*

That night, we sit in the courtyard, unwilling to be seen on the roof.

Mom holds Jesus on her lap and smothers him with kisses. "I'm going back to Bethlehem."

"Mom! No! We don't know what the soldiers are doing there."

"They came back this afternoon. Defeated. Word in the market is they killed all the baby boys." She pulls Jesus close to her chest.

Mary whispers, "Baby Ira. I have to go see Abi."

Mom shakes her head. "You need to get this one to Egypt. I'll take care of Abi and the others."

I dig through the treasures from the Parthians and hand her several gold coins. "If you run out before we return, promise me you'll go live with Sarah and her family."

She gives me a long hug. "I'll be okay."

That night, my dreams are plagued with sandstorms, thieves, and unscrupulous traders. I wake at midnight and go to the roof, searching the stars. *You used the stars to speak to men from Parthia. Show me something.*

The words of Isaiah fill my heart.

"Fear not, for I have redeemed you; I have called you by your name; you are Mine. When you pass through the waters, I will be with you; and through the rivers, they shall not overflow you. When you walk through the fire, you shall not be burned, nor shall the flame scorch you."[1]

I think of all Zechariah told me over the past few days. *I have a heritage of Hope. Yes, Lord, I choose Faith.*

I wake up to Amos shaking my shoulder. "It's time to go." He's wearing his travel cloak.

"Where are you going?"

"I know you don't trust me, and I don't blame you. But I can't leave you to figure out this trip alone. I've spent the past twenty years traveling, much of that in Egypt. Please, let me prove myself." He looks up at the temple. "Maybe, I can find a way to erase my guilt."

Where would we be if the Lord didn't change our hearts?

Zechariah walks with us to meet the merchant. He wraps Mary in a long hug. "What the Lord calls us to, He will bring us through."

"Thank you, Uncle. Tell Auntie I love her."

He embraces me. "The Lord bless you and keep you and be gracious to all of us. Go in peace."

A month later, I stand on the roof of my rented home in a Jewish community in Egypt. Jesus sleeps on my shoulder. Mary is at the market with her new friends. The familiar smells of fresh bread blend with the fragrance of new spices. I hear the men arguing in the synagogue a few streets away.

How many times have our people sought refuge here? Abraham, Isaac, Joseph, Jeremiah. But the Lord has always been faithful to bring us home.

I kiss the top of Jesus' head. He wraps his arms around my neck and mumbles something I don't quite hear.

Hope of Israel, help me to trust You.

---

1. Isaiah 43:1-2

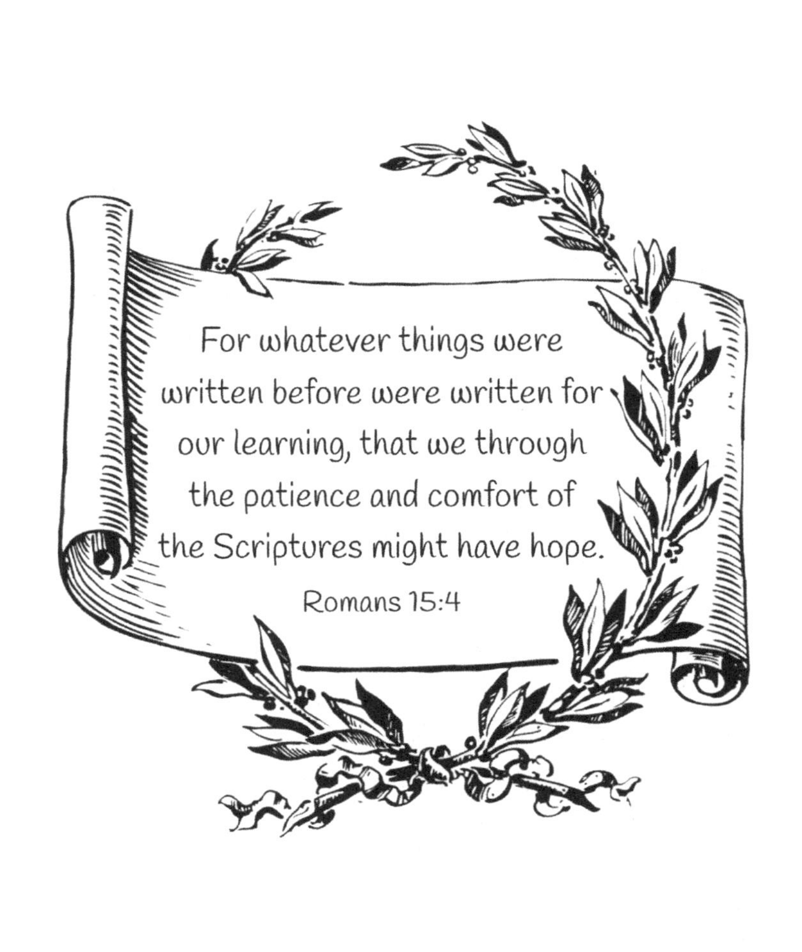
For whatever things were
written before were written for
our learning, that we through
the patience and comfort of
the Scriptures might have hope.
Romans 15:4

Know God

THANK YOU FOR SPENDING time with me. It could be, as you read this, you realized you don't know this Hope. Please allow me to introduce you.

The Bible tells us that everyone has sinned (Romans 3:23). Sin is anything we think, say, or do that is contrary to the righteousness of God. We all fall short of God's standard and, therefore, deserve death – eternal separation from God (Romans 6:23).

But God, in His great mercy and love, did not treat us as our sins deserve. While we were still caught up in our sin, before we could recognize our need for salvation, He put into place the plan He devised before the first man, Adam, committed the first sin.

God the Son (Jesus) put on a man suit. He set aside His glory, majesty, and power to become a baby. God became flesh and lived among us (John 1:14). He needed his diapers changed. He had to learn to walk and talk. He went through that awkward puberty stage. And, in all things, He aimed to please His Father in heaven (John 5:30). Twice, once at the beginning of His ministry (Mark 1:11), and once toward the end of His ministry (Matthew 17:5), God the Father speaks from heaven and declares that He is well-pleased with His Beloved Son. Everything Jesus thought, said, and did, pleased God the Father.

When the time was right, He set His face toward Jerusalem (Luke 9:51). Because He loves us and for the joy set before Him (our salvation), He endured the shame and suffering of death on a cross (Hebrews 12:2). But He didn't stay dead. Three days later, He proved He was God and stepped out of the tomb. He took 40 more days to teach His disciples before ascending to heaven where He sits, now, at the right hand of the Father.

He has already paid the price (death) for your sins. We can do nothing to earn His love or forgiveness. He freely offers it to everyone. We only need to receive it with repentance and thankfulness. If you are ready to receive His forgiveness, pray now and tell Him so. Then, find a church where they believe the Bible is the inspired word of God and that Jesus is God in the flesh and the only way of salvation. Get involved with a discipleship class there. Meet other believers, learn and grow with them.

And I would love it if you would send me a note telling me of your decision. Welcome to the Family.

Dig deeper into historical and cultrual context of

OUR STORIES

HOPE'S ARRIVAL

Go to **DeborahGatchel.com**
Select **blog**, then
A Way in a Manger
or scan the QR Code.

Our Stories

Hope's Arrival

Study Guide

Deborah Gatchel

Corpus Christi, TX

Contents

Timeline

THE BIBLE FOCUSES ON the events in and around Israel. But life was happening all across the globe. Cities were built and destroyed, inventions changed the world, and wars changed the political landscape. Here are a few events from the final Babylonian captivity through the intertestamental period.

All dates are BC

- 586 Jerusalem destroyed by Nebuchadnezzar, King of Babylon

- 539 Cyrus II issues a decree allowing Jews to return to Jerusalem

- 521 Persian palace built in Susa

- 516 Temple in Jerusalem is rebuilt

- 480 Battle of Thermopylae (Achaemenid Persian Empire under Xerxes I vs. an alliance of Greek city-states led by 300 Spartans under Leonidas I)

- ca. 480-470 Book of Esther

- 445 Nehemiah returns to Jerusalem

- 444 Walls of Jerusalem rebuilt

- ca. 400 Catapult invented
- ca. 350 Samaritans rebuild Shechem as a religious center
- 329 Alexander the Great conquers Jerusalem
- June 13, 323 Alexander the Great dies at the age of 32
- 301 After 22 years of fighting, Alexander's kingdom is divided into three parts, each ruled by one of his generals - Ptolemy in Egypt, Seleucus in Asia, and Antigonus in Macedonia. Judea sits on the border between the Ptolemaic and Seleucid empires and sees many territory battles.
- ca. 300 The Library of Alexandria is founded
- 312 Appian Way completed (Acts 28:15)
- 264 - 146 Punic Wars fought between Rome and Carthage (North Africa)
- 250 Parchment ("paper" made from sheep or goat skin) invented in Pergamum
- 200 Acropolis at Pergamum (Revelation 2:12) is built
- 168 Antiochus IV Epiphanes sets up a statue of Zeus in the Holy of Holies of the temple in Jerusalem
- 167 Maccabean (aka Hasmonean) revolt starts (see more info in "Anna & the Hasmoneans")
- 134 Maccabees gain independence

- 70 Amphitheater built in Rome
- 67 Pompey rids the Mediterranean of pirates
- June 63 Pompey conquers Jerusalem, desecrates the temple, and Judea becomes a Roman territory. A series of battles are fought to regain control of Jerusalem until Herod rises to power in 37.
- March 15, 44 Julius Caesar assassinated
- 40 Herod the Great declared King of the Jews but doesn't gain control of Jerusalem until 37. He banishes his first wife Doris and her child and marries Mariamne, a Hasmonean princess.
- 37 First public library built in Rome
- 31 Augustus Caesar begins to rule
- 27 Rome converts from a Republic to an Empire with Augustus Caesar as the first emperor
- ca. 29 Herod executes his Jewish wife Mariamne I
- 25 Rome gains control of Spain
- 25 Provence of Galatia founded
- 22 – 10 Herod builds Caesarea Maritime. This site becomes the Roman administrative center for Syria.
- 20 Herod builds a temple to Ceasar at the Cave of Pan in what will later be known as Ceasarea Philippi, north of the Sea of Galilee. (See Matthew 16:13, Mark 8:27)

- 20/19 Herod begins expanding the Temple in Jerusalem. Work continues long after his death, (until 63 AD), a mere seven years before its total destruction (See John 2:20)

ca. = *circa,* Latin for "about"

References:

- Logos Bible Study Timeline
- Biblehub.com timeline

Blessed be the God and Father of our Lord
Jesus Christ, who according to His abundant
mercy has begotten us again to a living
hope through the resurrection of Jesus Christ
from the dead, to an inheritance incorruptible
and undefiled and that does not fade
away, reserved in heaven for you, who are
kept by the power of God through faith for
salvation ready to be revealed in the last time.
1 Peter 1:3-5

Zechariah

Hope in the Faithful One

What do we know about Zechariah?

First, Luke wrote in Greek so Zechariah's name is a transliteration. Different translations have Zachariah, Zechariah, or Zacharias. Which spelling is correct? Any of them are possible, they're all the same person.

What do we know about Zechariah?

- He was a priest. Therefore, we know he was a descendant of Aaron.

- He was of the division of Abijah. David established 24 divisions of priests to serve in rotation at the temple (1 Chronicles 24). Tradition indicates that they served twice a year for one week at a time, plus during the three major festivals (Passover, First Fruits, and the Feast of Tabernacles). When the captives returned from Babylon, not all the courses, including Abijah's, were represented, so the larger groups filled in for the empty positions.

- He was righteous before God. In all manner of the Law, He sought to follow God.

- He and Elizabeth were childless, just like Abram and Sarai and Isaac and Rebecca. Children were considered the ultimate blessing from the Lord, so a man who had no children was considered cursed.

- He was "well advanced in years." Edersheim tells us this term was used for people over 60 years old. The Law forbids men over 50 to perform the sacrifices, but they may serve in supporting roles.

- Zechariah was chosen, by lot, to burn incense. This was the daily incense offered in the Holy Place. He was not the high priest, so he did not enter the Holy of Holies.

What we don't know

- We don't know what year the Luke 1 account occurred. We know it was at least two years before the death of King Herod (9 months for Elizabeth's pregnancy, an additional 6 months until the birth of Jesus, and probably 12-18 months before the Wise Men arrived). But when did King Herod die? That date is debated. Most scholars say either 4 or 1 B.C. Take your pick. People smarter than me with better access to the records can't figure it out.

- We don't know what month he was serving. A teaching is circulating that the announcement came during the Feast of Trumpets. Could be. It would be like God to give us that picture. But since we don't know what year, and we don't know, for sure, when each division served during that time, we have two (spring or fall) two-month windows to choose from and can't be positive.

We know a lot. And there's a lot of conjecture. We might build stories, but we must do so with the understanding that we are filling in with guesses. Our guesses and opinions must not become doctrine. Be gentle with those who have different guesses.

But the truth remains: God promised to send a forerunner to prepare the way for the Messiah. Elizabeth carried that prophet and provided a stepping stone of faith. If a woman well past the age of childbearing can know the joys of motherhood, it's not as far a leap to think that a virgin would conceive.

Hope in the Faithful One

As we walk through these stories, we'll get a better picture of life in Israel around the time Jesus was born. Their country had been ravaged by a century of war, only to be "rescued" by a paranoid king and ruled by an emperor who expected to be worshiped. But many, like Zechariah, clung to the promises of a messiah who would free them.

Most had a distorted view of his mission. But they knew God had promised and they trusted that He was faithful.

Dig Deeper

Read Hebrews 11.

What does Hebrews 11:1 mean?

Memorize three Bible verses about God's faithfulness. If you don't need them today, you will soon. Why did you choose these verses?

Carefully read about three of the people in Hebrews 11, or others in the Bible who showed great faith. Why did you choose them? What can you learn from their lives?

Who is someone you know who shows extraordinary faith?

Zechariah recited God's blessings and His promises, but when confronted with the fulfillment, it was too wonderful for him to believe. When do you find it difficult to have faith? Are there things you've asked God for that, maybe, you're beginning to doubt His ability or willingness to do?

Zechariah was righteous, but when an angel from God stood before him and made him a promise, he doubted. Was it because it was outside the bounds of natural law? Or was it because it struck a raw nerve of unmet hope? Do you have areas where you are afraid to let God make you big promises?

Pray

Jesus, thank You for all Your promises and for being faithful to fulfill them. Teach me to walk in a deeper faith in You.

Mary

Hope in Obedience

Women in Israel

The Israelites were a patriarchal society. Men had the authority, took leadership roles, and fought the battles. Modern teachings have proposed that women were second-class citizens, treated inferior to men. A study of Jewish literature will show that was not the case.

Many sections in Proverbs show women as treasures. And God-fearing women are always held in high esteem. Several Levitical laws give special protections for women, even those laws that seem odious to our Western minds.

> Read Who Hast Not Made Me a Woman on Torah.org for the perspective from a modern Jewess from an Israeli community on the role of women in scripture. Find a direct link at HopesArrival.com.

So, what was the state of women?

At the time of Christ, most young women were betrothed around twelve years of age, when they hit puberty. The betrothal ceremony was a legal contract between the families, often relatives. The young girl had the right of refusal. Some sources say this was truly her right, others insist it was a mere formality and she was expected to adhere to her father's wishes.

Once engaged, she was considered married, though the wedding ceremony would be held about a year later. When the wedding day arrived, she would be taken to her husband's father's house. The wedding feast, attended by friends and family, could last a week. At some point during this week, the marriage was consummated. The young couple would live with the groom's family, rather than in their own home.

> Read more at My Jewish Learning, Ancient Jewish Marriage

As in most agrarian societies, women were needed to run the home. Without the convenience of the local mall and grocery store, feeding and clothing a family was a full-time job.

Making bread, the staple of their diet, took two to three hours each day. The wife began early in the morning, gathering thorns, sticks, and animal dung to make the fire. Then she had to hand-grind the grain, mix it with water and salt, and a bit of fermented yeast. Finally, she formed it into loaves and slapped it on the inside wall of the oven to cook.

And water? Each day, she took her pitcher to the local well or spring to fill it and carried it home for all the family's cooking and cleaning needs.

Clothing was no easier. Once the sheep were sheared, she had to clean and card the wool, spin it into thread, and wind it onto the spindle. From there, she would weave it into cloth and sew it into clothing.

Additionally, there would have been a family garden, helping as needed during harvest, and the many other tasks of running a household.

But her primary responsibility was the bearing and raising of children to honor the Lord. Children are a blessing from the Lord, and a Jewish home, filled with lively children was considered the greatest blessing. Only a righteous and wise wife and mother could fulfill such duties.

What do we know about Mary?

Mary would have been raised with the expectation of filling these roles. What else do we know about her?

The Bible tells us she:

- was a virgin
- lived in Nazareth
- was engaged to Joseph
- was a close relative of Elizabeth, a "daughter of Aaron," so she must have also been of a priestly line, probably through her mother's side
- presented Jesus at the Temple and offered her purification sacrifice
- offered the purification sacrifice of a poor woman
- spent time in Egypt to protect her Son

- went to Jerusalem for the Passover Feast
- worried when she lost Jesus in Jerusalem
- witnessed the crucifixion of her Son
- joined the apostles for prayer during the ten days between Jesus' ascension and the Day of Pentecost

In Cana, she knew Jesus could solve the lack of wine at the wedding feast. (John 2:1-12)

When we see her in Mark 3:31-35, Jesus won't acknowledge her. Is that because His brothers had convinced her that He was out of His mind? (Mark 3:21)

Interesting side note: Mary was a shortened form of Mariamme, the name of the Hasmonean princess who Herod married and later murdered.* Mary became a popular name among those protesting the Roman occupation of Judea.

*Read more about the Hasmoneans in the notes about Anna.

Hope in Obedience

We don't know what Mary was like. Was she outgoing, or did she prefer solitude? Was she a natural leader or would she rather be at the back of the room? The Bible doesn't say. But we know she found favor with God (Luke 1:30). From that one statement, and her response, "Behold, the maidservant of the Lord! Let it be to me according to your word" (Luke 1:38), we can guess that she had cultivated a habit of obedience. She was probably about 13 years old, no more than 15 years. But when God called her to do the impossible, she had an anchor of obedience and trust in her Lord that put faith in her heart and the right response in her mouth.

Dig Deeper

Read Esther.

Go back and read Esther 4:15-16. Esther had to choose: safety and comfort or risk her life to protect her people and stand against unrighteousness. In Hebrews 11, we read about many who died standing for God. God's desire for us is that we willingly obey and give Him our "yes." What areas do you find it easy to say "yes" to God? Where are you reluctant to trust Him?

Memorize three verses about obedience or sacrifice. Why did you choose these verses?

Find three people in the Bible who obeyed. Read their stories. Why did you choose them? What can you learn from their lives?

Who is someone you know who consistently obeys God?

Read Galatians 2:20. How many personal pronouns (I, me, my) are in that verse? Grammatically, it's a self-centered verse, but conceptually, it exemplifies the Christ-life. Break down and explain each phrase in this verse.

Mary knew what could happen when it was discovered that she was pregnant, yet she gave God her "yes." What is one area you are holding back from God? Where do you need to tell Him, "yes." If you can't think of something, spend time in prayer and truthful consideration. We all have areas where we must surrender more to Jesus.

Pray

Jesus, thank You for giving Yourself for me. Help me to live each day to honor and to serve You. I give You my "yes."

Elizabeth

Hope Going Through

What do we know about Elizabeth?

- Elizabeth was a daughter of Aaron. The Law presented strict guidelines about who a priest could marry. While being of priestly descent was not a requirement for a wife, extra blessings were thought to follow a couple who both were of the Aaronic line.

- She was righteous before God. In all manner of the Law, she sought to follow God.

- She and Zechariah were childless, just like Abram and Sarai and Isaac and Rebecca. Children were considered the ultimate blessing from the Lord, so a man who had no children was considered cursed.

- She and Zechariah were both well advanced in years. Edersheim tells us this term was used for people over 60 years old.

- Since they had to motion to Zechariah to confirm John's name (Luke 1:62), we can infer that he was deaf as well as mute. She could not share her fears and frustrations with him.

- She shared the same name as the wife of Aaron, brother of Moses, the first High Priest.

We don't know how much time passed between Gabriel's announcement and when Elizabeth became pregnant. Was Zechariah at the beginning or end of his time of service? Did Elizabeth need to have a period and start the reproductive cycle after he got home, or had God miraculously prepared her womb? Did she get pregnant immediately, or did it take several months? We don't know.

But this we do know: God promised to send a forerunner to prepare the way for the Messiah. Elizabeth carried that prophet and provided a stepping stone of faith. If a woman well past the age of childbearing can know the joys of motherhood, it's not as far a leap to think that a virgin would conceive.

Hope Going Through

Read Psalm 23.

Look at Psalm 23:4. "Even though I walk through the valley of the shadow of death." David expects to go through difficult times. He understands that they are part of life. He says, in that valley, "Your rod and Your staff comfort me." They are included in "everything I need."

The shepherd's rod was protection. He used it to fight off wild animals that came after the sheep. Sometimes we're in The

Valley because of outside dangers. We find comfort in His rod, knowing He will always protect us.

The staff was correction. He used it to guide the sheep and, when one wandered off, he could use the crook to grab around the neck and pull her back. Sometimes we go through The Valley because we've wandered. His staff comforts us by pulling us back to His safety.

But, whatever we do, we must go through. Don't stop in the middle.

Dig Deeper

Read the stories of three people in the Bible who went through difficult times. Were their problems because of disobedience or outside dangers? What did they do to keep going?

Memorize three verses to help you remember to trust God when things are hard.

Elizabeth lived with one of the most excruciating pains a Hebrew woman could endure. Many women know the pain of infertility. Elizabeth had the added stigma from Jewish culture regarding a barren woman. How many whispers did she hear? "If she were truly righteous, she'd have children." "God is punishing her for something." "I can't believe Zechariah hasn't divorced her. They must be hiding something."

Yet, she maintained her faith and continued to live righteously through the valley. I'm sure she expected to die in the valley. But she trusted the rod and the staff, and the Lord Who held them and she emerged with a testimony that is being repeated 2,000 years later.

What valley are you in or have you recently been through? Were you guided by the rod or the staff? What helped you go through? What testimony do you have because of the valley?

Pray

Jesus, I trust You, the Good Shepherd. Thank You for Your rod and Your staff. Help me to trust and find comfort in both and to continue through each valley, walking out with a greater testimony of Your faithfulness.

Mary's Father

Encouraging Hope

The two lineages of Jesus

MATTHEW 1:1-17 AND LUKE 3:23-38 both record the genealogy of Jesus.

But they list different ancestors.

Who's right? Who made a mistake? Does the Bible contradict itself?

I propose the following answers: Both, no one, and absolutely not.

Jesus had two parents and four grandparents, so two genealogies would not represent a contradiction.

Let's look at the two Gospels, and then discuss what might be happening.

Matthew was written by Matthew, the tax collector and disciple of Jesus. His Gospel is written for a primarily Jewish audience and references the Old Testament more than any other Gospel. He records Jesus' ancestors beginning with Abraham, through David and the kingly line to Jacob then Joseph.

Luke was a physician who accompanied Paul on his journeys. His books, Luke and Acts, are the only ones verifiably written by a Gentile. His gospel carefully explains the Jewish histories and traditions for a non-Jewish audience. His genealogy begins with Joseph and Heli, and traces through David back to Adam.

So, why the different genealogies? The most generally accepted explanation is that Matthew records Joseph's line, focusing on the heritage of David, while Luke records Mary's to emphasize the virgin birth.

But wait! It says Joseph was the son of Heli. How is that Mary's line?

Good question. I'm glad you asked. It shows you are reading critically.

To answer that question, let's go back to Numbers 26 and 27. Moses is giving instructions on how the land is to be divided: each tribe is to receive an allotment, then each man in that tribe will receive a portion.

A man named Zelophehad had five daughters who approached Moses with a petition. They had no brothers, and their father had died in the wilderness. Would their father lose his portion of the inheritance because he didn't have a son?

Moses, stumped, asked God. God answered that, if a man has no sons, his daughters would become heirs, with his sons-in-law essentially being adopted into his family.

Did Mary have any brothers? We don't know. But, if she didn't, it would answer all the questions. Heli would be Mary's father who adopted Joseph as his heir. This is the scenario I chose to represent in Joseph's and Mary's father's stories.

Encouraging Hope

The Bible doesn't tell us about Mary's family's reaction to the news of her pregnancy, but we can guess that she didn't say anything before she went "with haste" to see Elizabeth. Then, for three months, Mary sat with Elizabeth. They ground grain, made bread, cooked, and cleaned together. And they talked like women do. They had three months to encourage each other so when Mary returned home, she was prepared to face the shame. She didn't know what would happen. But she knew the Lord would be with her through it.

Dig Deeper

Read 1 Samuel 30.

Look at 1 Samuel 30:6. David and his men just marched three days with the Philistine King Achish to go to battle against King Saul. The other Philistine kings refused to fight with David, so he and his men packed up and marched three days back to their city – only to find it burned and their families gone. In addition to being tired and grieving for his family, David had to bear the anger of all his men. That's a heavy burden. But he encouraged himself in the Lord.

The word "encourage" breaks down to "speak courage into." Who is encouraging you? Who is speaking courage into your life? Who do you draw your courage and strength from?

Memorize three verses about finding encouragement in Jesus Christ. Why did you choose these verses?

Read the stories of three people in the Bible who showed courage. Where did they find their courage?

Who do you know who is a good encourager? What things do they say? How do they say it?

Who do you know who shows courage? What is their source of strength?

Where can you grow in courage? Who can help encourage you?

Write a letter to someone who needs encouragement. Be specific about addressing their needs. Make sure to share our true source of Strength and Hope with them.

Pray

Jesus, I praise You, my Courage and my Strength. Without you, I can do nothing, but when You give me strength, I can do all things. Help me to keep my focus on You to boldly do what You have called me to.

Joseph

Hope in Shame

Who was Joseph?

THE BIBLE TELLS US:

- He was of the house of David (Luke 1:27, Luke 2:4, Matthew 1:20)
- He was betrothed to Mary (Luke 1:27, Matthew 1:18)
- When he went to Jerusalem to redeem Jesus, he offered the sacrifice of a poor person (Luke 2:24; Leviticus 12:8)
- He raised Jesus in Nazareth (Luke 2:39)
- He went to Jerusalem every year for the Feast of Passover (Luke 2:41)
- He was a just man (Matthew 1:19)
- He believed the angels (Matthew 1:20-21, 24; 2:13, 22-23)

What was Joseph's occupation?

The Greek word translated "carpenter" means "builder" or "architect." In Joseph's day, buildings were made of stone, not wood, so he likely was a stone mason. See Associates for Biblical Research: Jesus the "Tekton"

Where was Joseph from?

From Nazareth, of course!

Really? Let's look carefully at the text:

Matthew 2:1 Now after Jesus was born in Bethlehem of Judea in the days of Herod the king...

- Jesus was born in Bethlehem
- The wise men found the young child (toddler) in Bethlehem

Matthew 2:22-23 But when he heard that Archelaus was reigning over Judea instead of his father Herod, he was afraid to go there. And being warned by God in a dream, he turned aside into the region of Galilee. And he came and dwelt in a city called Nazareth....

- Bethlehem is in Judea
- When returning from Egypt, their first plan was to go to Bethlehem. Nazareth was Plan B.

Luke 1:26-27 Now in the sixth month the angel Gabriel was sent by God to a city of Galilee named Nazareth, to a virgin betrothed to a man whose name was Joseph, of the house of David. The virgin's name was Mary.

- Mary was from Nazareth

Luke 2:4-5 Joseph also went up from Galilee, out of the city of Nazareth, into Judea, to the city of David, which is called Bethlehem, because he was of the house and lineage of David, to be registered with Mary, his betrothed wife, who was with child.

- Under the Roman tax system, men had to register where they held property. Joseph had to go to Bethlehem.

Luke 2:39 So when they had performed all things according to the law of the Lord, they returned to Galilee, to their city, Nazareth.

- This passage immediately follows Jesus' dedication at the temple in Jerusalem. But if we mesh the timeline with Matthew, they had to have returned to Nazareth after the Wise Men's visit and the flight to Egypt.

Luke 2:51 Then He went down with them and came to Nazareth, and was subject to them

- This verse follows Jesus' extended visit to Jerusalem when he was 12 years old.

Nowhere does either author say that Joseph was from Nazareth. From Luke 2:4, we might infer that he was living there, since he went from Nazareth to Bethlehem on account of the census. But not necessarily. For the wedding, the groom would take the bride to his home. Maybe he went to Nazareth to take Mary to Bethlehem for the wedding, and the census was just tied up in that. From Luke's detailed accounts, I'm going to guess not, but we must keep that in mind as a possibility.

After Jesus' birth, the family stayed in Bethlehem until they went to Egypt. Or maybe they returned to Nazareth after the dedication, as Luke records, then, later returned to Bethlehem. (Unlikely, but possible.) Either way, Bethlehem was a place that Joseph was comfortable staying.

When they returned from Egypt, their first inclination was to go to Bethlehem. That would only make sense if Bethlehem was "home."

I present the possibility that Joseph was not *from* Nazareth. He may have been *staying* in Nazareth for some reason, but his home was in Bethlehem.

Hope in Shame

Joseph faced an excruciating decision. If he took Mary as his wife, everyone would "know" that he was the baby's father. If he didn't, Mary would live a life of shame or be stoned to death. He took her shame on himself. What a beautiful foreshadowing of what his Son would do for him and all of us.

Dig Deeper

Read 2 Samuel 6.

Reread 2 Samuel 6:20-22. As David danced and twirled before the Lord, his robes flew up, exposing him in a manner that would be considered shameful under other circumstances. Michal focused on the indignity. David focused on the Lord.

While we must use wisdom when making decisions, sometimes, God's wisdom places us in situations that will be awkward or bring embarrassment.

The Bible tells the stories of many people who ended up in shameful situations (jail, cast out, mocked, beaten) because they chose to honor God. Find three of the stories and read them. Why did you choose them? What common themes do you see in their lives?

Memorize three verses about honoring God. Why did you choose these verses?

What are the limits of mocking and disgrace that you are willing to endure for Jesus? Where do you draw back? What holds you back? What can you focus on to help you walk more boldly in Jesus Christ?

Pray

Jesus, thank You for enduring the shame of the cross for me. I was the joy that caused You to endure. Help me to endure shame and suffering for Your name.

Joseph's Mother

Hope in His Righteousness

Traditions

THIS CHAPTER MAY HAVE upended many of your traditions. Thank you for sticking with me.

What are traditions? Why do we have them? Should we have them?

Miriam Webster defines tradition as "an inherited, established, or customary pattern of thought, action, or behavior (such as a religious practice or a social custom)." Every family, community, and religion has its traditions. Some are unique, many are shared with others.

Traditions anchor us to our past and give us a sense of belonging. They provide predictable patterns for our lives and, during times of upheaval, can give us a breath of normalcy.

The Books of Exodus, Leviticus, and Numbers all focus on establishing traditions. These God-ordained patterns and thoughts are still clung to 3,500 years later, uniting the Jewish community in a shared past, future, and identity. We see that some traditions are good.

When Jesus rebuked the religious leaders of His time, it often concerned their traditions, specifically the ones that went contrary to what God had established. But He fully participated in other celebrations not outlined in the Law such as a wedding feast and the Feast of Dedication (now known as Hanukkah).

Jesus and the apostles established traditions for the Church including Communion, meeting together regularly, and certain songs and hymns. (See 2 Thessalonians 2:15) These keep us focused on our identity in Jesus and the Hope of His coming.

Based on Jesus' example, I think we can state that traditions are good, as long as our traditions align with, or don't contradict, scripture. They create a sense of belonging and give us hope for the future. But, as with everything else, we must compare them to the plumbline of the Word of God.

Hope in His Righteousness

When the Law said, "Remember the Sabbath Day by keeping it Holy," the Scribes and Pharisees outlined myriads of laws dictating what that looks like. You may only travel 2,000 cubits (a little more than half a mile) from your home. You may do no work, not even lift a mat, unless it is to save a human life. These are the traditions Jesus spoke against and we find Him frequently breaking.

In this story, Joseph's mom sought to be a good mom following traditions and expectations, but her disbelief kept her from seeing the savior in her own home.

Dig Deeper

Read Matthew 5-7.

Reread Matthew 5:20. The scribes and Pharisees were proud of their righteousness. In the "Sermon on the Mount," Jesus shows how their outward deeds were insufficient. True righteousness is not about "doing," it's about the condition of our hearts.

Memorize three verses about true righteousness.

When we focus on our works, it's easy to compare ourselves with others and either think "I'm not as bad as him!" or "I can never be like her." This kind of thinking distorts our view of who we are in Jesus Christ.

What is your identity in Jesus Christ? If you have trusted Him to forgive your sins and give you a new life, then you have His righteousness. Do you live like it? Or do you compare yourself with others?

When we understand our righteousness in Jesus Christ, we can be secure in our calling and will have an honest response when we come under correction.

Pray

Jesus, thank You for giving me Your Righteousness. Help me to see myself as You see me, someone You loved enough to give Your life for.

The Shepherd

Proclaiming His Hope

Who were the shepherds?

Ask the Internet, and you'll discover that the shepherds were outcasts, unwelcome in the synagogue and temple. But also, they were special priests in charge of special sheep designated for the temple sacrifice. And they were most definitely children, because the adults were too busy tending the fields. But they were absolutely men, strong enough to defend the flocks against wild animals and thieves. And it 100% was not December, because it would be too cold for sheep to be out. But we know that the sheep of that area are bred for the colder weather and they lamb in December, plus it's not really that cold in Bethlehem in December. And winter, when there were no crops in the ground, was the only time the shepherds would have their sheep in the tilled fields.

So, that didn't help. What can we glean from scripture?

In Luke 2, we see that they were shepherds, in the fields near Bethlehem. The Greek doesn't even say they were in the fields. It says they were camping out.

In Luke 2:17-18, we see the shepherds telling everyone what they saw. And everyone was totally amazed that the Lord would reveal Himself to repulsive shepherds. **Nope**. They were amazed at the shepherds' report. Apparently, they believed the shepherds and weren't shocked that God chose to tell them.

Furthermore, in John 10, Jesus refers to Himself as the Good Shepherd and Mark 6:34 says Jesus had compassion on the crowd because they were like sheep without a shepherd. In Luke 15:3-7, Jesus says, "Suppose one of you [it could be any of them] has a hundred sheep [having a hundred sheep would make one a shepherd] and loses one of them. Doesn't he leave the ninety-nine in the open country and go after the lost sheep until he finds it?"

None of these references cast shepherds in a bad light. In fact, Jesus seems to portray them nobly. I think we can strike out "unwelcome outcasts."

I'm going to leave the priest for another day, but the short answer is, no. There is no record of special sheep or priestly shepherds in any literature written within 1,000 years of Jesus' birth. The best I can tell, the story of the priestly shepherds and special flocks was started by an author in the late 1800s. This man took a section of the Talmud, Jewish commentaries compiled in Babylon 300 years after Christ, pulled it out of context and made it say something that even a cursory reading of the original would refute. We'll leave it there for now.

So, who were the shepherds? David was a shepherd as a young man, not old enough for military service. Rachel and Zipporah were shepherdesses. Amos and Moses were shepherds as adults. How many of these were abnormal? We don't know. But there's hardly enough evidence to make a rule about any of them and certainly we can't exclude any of these groups.

Since we don't have firm Scriptural evidence in any direction, let's take a look at the culture and see what we can deduce.

- Israel was an agricultural society in the time of Christ.
- Property, including sheep, passed from father to son. Also, a son generally worked in his father's business, learning the trade from him.
- Most families, also, had land that needed tilled, planted, then harvested. Many also had another family business.

So, let's paint a possible picture. Shepherding was a family business. As such, usually, the task of taking care of the sheep fell to the men and boys. Maybe it was the young teens, old enough to fight off animals, but not strong enough to help with the fields and the bee hives (or tannery, or the potter's wheel). Maybe it was a full-time family affair, and mostly everyone worked together, but Grandpa kept watch over the young 'uns when the men had to take care of the field. We may never know for sure.

But they were in the fields, faithfully doing their job. And God sent the angels to proclaim "good tidings of great joy" for all of them, and all of us.

Proclaiming His Hope

The shepherds told everyone what they had heard about Jesus, and everyone marveled (Luke 2:17-18). What had they been told? "For there is born to you this day in the city of David a Savior, who is Christ the Lord" (Luke 2:11).

As the angel said, that's good tidings of great joy, for all people (Luke 2:10).

We have Good News. We have the Hope the world needs. He heals the brokenhearted, frees the captives, and consoles those who mourn.

Dig Deeper

At the beginning of His ministry, Jesus read Isaiah 61:1-2 in the synagogue, then proclaimed Himself the fulfillment of that prophecy.

Read Isaiah 61, being mindful of Who it says Jesus is.

What Hope do these promises offer you? Let them sink into your heart and soul. Know that He will do what He has promised.

Memorize three verses about Jesus, our Hope. Why did you choose these verses?

Pray for the people you know. Who needs this message of Hope? Pray for an opportunity to share this Hope with them.

Pray

Jesus, thank You for being my Hope. Help me to share Your Hope and Freedom with those around me.

Simeon

Hope in the Waiting

Who was Simeon?

A COUPLE DAYS AFTER Jesus' birth, Mary and Joseph travel to Jerusalem to offer a sacrifice. There, they meet an old prophet who speaks blessings over Jesus and then he goes home and dies. At least that's how I understood the story when I was a child.

What really happened?

The Law of Moses required parents to redeem their firstborn with a specific sacrifice, 40 days after birth. This redemption ties back to the first Passover in Egypt when God spared the firstborn of the obedient Israelites. Mary and Joseph, being righteous, obeyed the law, traveled to Jerusalem, and presented the offering required of poor families.

While they were there (before or after the sacrifice, the Bible doesn't say), Simeon approaches them and, taking Jesus in his arms, prophecies over him. His blessing contained some harsh words. "He will be a sign that is spoken against." And to Mary, "A sword will pierce your soul." Redemption carries a heavy price. I wonder if Joseph and Mary ever had a twinge of regret at being chosen.

The Bible does NOT say that he was an old man. We assume he was because, when he held Jesus, he said, "Lord, now You are letting Your servant depart in peace, according to Your word." These sound like the words of an old man. But, maybe he was middle-aged and his life was fulfilled. Or, maybe He was plagued with an ailment and was tired of fighting. Or, maybe he was old.

Hope in the Waiting

We do know he was waiting for the Consolation of Israel, as many were in his day. Caesar Augustus brought peace to the Roman empire but at a high cost for a monotheistic nation. The Jewish community was divided between those who welcomed the peace and security brought by the Roman governance and those who despised the pagan influence and intrusion into their lives.

We don't know how long Simeon had been waiting, but his expression of thanksgiving indicates that it had been some time. Since he remained faithful to the Lord through the waiting, he joined the shepherds and Anna as one of three witnesses proclaiming the birth of the Messiah (See Deuteronomy 19:15).

Fill in the details however we may, his story is a beautiful testimony of the blessings of those who wait with expectation for the fulfillment of the Lord's promises.

Dig Deeper

Read Psalm 27. David declares his trust in the Lord but is honest about his circumstances. It feels like he's looking back and forth – life is hard, but I will trust God. Problems keep coming, but God will deliver me. We see the faith he has developed, waiting for God through many years of hardship.

Memorize three verses about waiting for the Lord in Hope. Hint: look at the Psalms.

David was a teenager when Samuel anointed him to be king of Israel. He didn't take the throne until he was 30 years old. That's a lot of waiting. List some of the problems he had to endure while he waited. How did he handle them?

What promises of God are you waiting on? How are you handling the waiting?

Pray

Lord Jesus, thank You for Your promises and Your faithfulness to do everything you have said. Teach me to focus on You and to Hope in Your faithfulness through the waiting.

Anna

Hope for Rededication

What do we know about Anna?

SHE GETS THREE VERSES in the Bible (Luke 2:36-38). From them we know:

- She was a prophetess
- Her father (or more distant ancestor) was Phanuel of the tribe of Asher
- Her husband died 7 years after their marriage
- She was about 84 years old*
- She lived in the temple day and night. There is no record of dwelling places in Herod's Temple. My archaeologist friends suggest that she slept just outside the gates.
- She was dedicated to the Lord and served Him with fasting and prayer
- She testified of Jesus to all who looked for redemption in Jerusalem.

When I started praying about Anna's story, I asked, "Why didn't she remarry? What happened at the time of her husband's death?"

A few calculations put her husband's death around 60 BC. What happened in that timeframe? Pompey laid siege to Jerusalem in 63, effectively ending the Hasmonean dynasty.

What was the Hasmonean Dynasty? Their story is recorded in the apocryphal books of Maccabees, so most Catholics are familiar with them. Let's have a brief history lesson for us Protestants who missed out.

After Alexander the Great died, his kingdom was divided into three parts, each ruled by one of his generals. Jerusalem was on the dividing line between two of these regions. For a long time, the powers that were, happily let Jerusalem be a buffer state. Occasionally, one group would conquer the other and it would switch hands, but mostly, they were on their own.

In the late second century BC, there came a Seleucid ruler, Antiochus IV Epiphanes, who distrusted the split loyalties of the Jews and outlawed the practice of Judaism. He desecrated the temple, set up a statue of Zeus in the Holy of Holies, and sent his soldiers to the surrounding villages to force people to sacrifice pigs to the Greek gods. In a little village north of Jerusalem, a priest named Mattathias Hashmon refused to offer the required sacrifice. When another villager stepped forward for the task, Mattathias killed him and the soldier, sparking the Hasmonean revolt, led by Mattathias and his five sons.

Three years later, the Hasmoneans (also known as the Maccabees) gained control of Jerusalem. They celebrated the rededication of the temple in the month of Kislev (December) and commemorated it in an annual festival called the Feast of Dedication in John 10, now known as Hanukkah.

Fighting continued for another twenty-five years until the Jews drove out their enemies and gained full independence. Simon, the only surviving son of Mattathias, set himself up as King and High Priest, though he was of neither David's nor Aaron's line. He and his descendants ruled Israel for 80 years until two brothers, Hyrcanus and Aristobulus, disputed over their right to the throne.

By this time, international power had shifted to the Romans. Both brothers sent a delegation to the Roman general Pompey requesting his support. A third party also courted Pompey asking him to remove the Hasmoneans, entirely.

Pompey responded by taking control of Jerusalem in 63 BC. A thousand rebels barricaded themselves in the Temple with the priests. After a three-month siege, Pompey broke through the wall and slaughtered all 12,000 men inside. During the siege and the subsequent battle, the priests didn't stop their duties until they were struck down.

For the next 30 years, Jerusalem was the site of many battles as different factions tried to regain control. Hyrcanus was allowed to rule as a puppet ethnarch (local ruler within an empire) until 47 BC when Julius Ceasar appointed Antipater as procurator of Judea. In 30 BC, Caesar Agustus named Antipater's son, Herod (the Great), King of the Jews. Herod married a Hasmonean princess to solidify his right to the throne.

Historians tell us that Herod fluctuated between periods of magnificent building projects and bouts of paranoia. He had his sons and wife killed in a jealous fit. As he lay on his deathbed, he commanded 100 priests to be confined to his palace and executed at the time of his death so the people would mourn. Thankfully, his daughter intervened and freed the priests.

Our friend Anna lived as a widow through years of battles, learning to hear the voice of the Lord and finding refuge in His Presence in the Temple.

*Another possible translation is that Anna was a widow for 84 years, which would put her well over 100. So, I favor the other translation.

Hope for Rededication

Just as, after Antiochus defiled the temple, it had to be purified and rededicated, God requires His people to be pure and holy. We must be cleansed and yield our whole selves to Him. Anything less is idolatry.

But the Good News is, we don't have to labor to yield and dedicate ourselves to Him. His Spirit in us gives us the strength and power to love Him as He requires. It's a Divine initiative with a Divine response. We only need to learn to walk in the Love He has planted in us.

Dig Deeper

Read Matthew 22:34-40.

The Pharisees added requirements to ensure people obeyed the Law. Jesus took the whole Law and all the teachings of the Prophets and summed them up in two commands: Love God with all your heart, soul, and mind and love your neighbor as yourself. Rather than following a growing list of rules, Jesus said God desires our hearts, soul, and minds dedicated to Him.

Memorize three scripture verses about dedication or rededication to God. Why did you choose these?

Several times, the Israelites walked away from God and then repented and rededicated themselves. Find five times where this happened. Why did they walk away? What caused them to repent? Why do you think they kept wandering?

We are different from the Israelites because we have the Spirit of Christ living in us as a constant source of strength.

Are there areas where you struggle to remain faithful to God? What draw does that sin hold over you? Is there something you are feeding your spirit that invites that sin? If so, cut it out. Then, knowing that those who are in Christ are not bound by sin, spend time repenting, acknowledging your dependence on Jesus, and asking for His Presence to fill you, leaving no room for the sinful desires.

Pray

Jesus, thank You for Your gentle Spirit Who leads us to repentance and constantly draws us closer to You. Help me to love You with all my heart, with all my soul, with all my mind, and with all my strength.

The Wise Man

Hope in God's Wisdom

Who were the Wise Men?

THE BIBLE TELLS US they:

- were from the East,
- came to Jerusalem to worship the King of the Jews,
- had seen His star in the East,
- fell down and worshiped Him,
- brought treasures for gifts: gold, frankincense, and myrrh,
- had a divine dream telling them not to return to Herod, and
- obeyed the dream.

The Greek word used to name them, *magoi*, has nothing to do with their level of discernment. They likely were astrologers, royal advisors, or possibly magicians in whatever country they came from.

What we don't know about the wise men:

- How many there were. The Bible uses the plural, so there were at least two.

- Where they were from. We know somewhere east of Jerusalem. There's a lot of land east of Jerusalem.

- Where they saw the star. The Greek word for "East" means "rising," as in the place the sun rises. "We saw his star in the East" could simply mean, "We're from the East, we saw it at home." Or, it could mean, "We saw it when it rose." Or, "We saw it in the eastern sky."

- Their religion or previous experience with the God of the Jews. They recognized the sign in the stars that a king had been born. We have no indication that they recognized His Deity.

Let's talk about the star.

- The Wise men saw the star either in the East or at its rising.

- After they left Jerusalem, the star went before them, until it came and stood over where the young Child was.

- When they saw the star in Jerusalem, they rejoiced with exceedingly great joy. *Note: The Bible does NOT say they followed the star or that they tracked it from the east.*

- The Greek word for "star" can be used for any heavenly body: stars, planets, asteroids, or comets.

- We don't know which of these it was, or if it was a supernatural phenomenon.

This story was the most difficult for me to write because I wanted to paint an accurate picture, but with so many unknowns, it is impossible to definitively form a picture. I landed on an obscure fact from Jewish history and created their story from there. As far as I know, it has not been seriously considered as an explanation of the Wisemen's identity and I do not claim that it holds any scholarly merit.

But, for the love of history, let's look at the *exilarches*.

The Parthian Empire (247 BC – 224 AD) included the office of "exilarch," representing Jews in government business. The first records of this office are from the second century AD, but Jewish tradition dates it 500 years earlier to King Jehoiachin's release from prison by the Babylonian King Evil-merodach (Jeremiah 52:31-34). The exilarches claimed to be descendants of King Jehoiachin, making them heirs to his throne and considered kings in waiting.

Did the office last that long? Through those five centuries, the region was ruled by the:

1. Babylonians

2. Persians

3. Greeks (Alexander the Great died in Nebuchadnezzar's palace)

4. Seleucids

5. Parthians

That's a long time and a lot of government changes for such an office to be maintained. However, we know from Ezra, Nehemiah, and the later prophets that there were several influential Jews in the Persian empire. We know that Jerusalem was a buffer state in the boundary war between the Seleucids and the Ptolemaic Empire in Egypt. That same battle continued between Rome and the Parthians, with slightly different boundaries. I can see where having favor with the resident Jews could be politically beneficial for both these empires. And, even without a government-sponsored role, it would be likely that the Jews established such leadership within their community.

So, what if these men, learned in the Law and the Prophets, and with the Babylonian knowledge of the stars, saw a particular star where it didn't belong? And they knew it signaled the fulfillment of prophecy. What would you do?

Read more about the Exilarches at HopesArrival.com

Hope in God's Wisdom

Many powerful and intelligent people have their own ideas about how the world should run. And, since God doesn't do things their way, they decide He must not exist or that He is foolish or unjust.

We, who have the Wisdom of God, must pray for them, that their eyes would be opened to the Truth.

Dig Deeper

Read 1 Corinthians 1:14-31. This section is written in classic Pauline logic. Read it several times, slowly so you understand the message. Use a simpler translation such as the New Century Version or the New Living Translation if that will help you.

Sum up this passage in two or three sentences.

Find five stories in the Bible about a time when God's instructions didn't make sense. Did the people obey? What happened?

God's wisdom ensures we learn to trust Him. When the Israelites marched around Jericho and the walls fell, there is no way anyone could think it was Joshua's military strength that won the victory. Every Israelite saw the power of God and had Hope that they could conquer the land.

Write about a time you needed God's Wisdom and He showed you what to do. Share your story with a friend or family member.

Pray

Jesus, I praise You as the Wisdom of God. Your plan is perfect and trustworthy, and I can hope in You.

The Scribe

Hope in Hard Choices

Who were the scribes?

Jesus often lumped the scribes and Pharisees together in condemnation. What was so special about them to warrant such treatment?

Jewish boys began their education around six years old. They learned to read and write Hebrew and instruction was almost exclusively in the Torah for the express purpose of being able to read and discuss scripture.

Scribes continued their education to include a deeper study of the Law of Moses and the art of asking questions. While Jesus often referred to them with the Pharisees, they were distinct from them. The Pharisees were a religious sect that held tightly to the traditions with strict adherence to the Law. Because of their mutual love for making rules, many Scribes were also Pharisees. But, while the Pharisees were religious leaders, the Scribes held an official office. Every town employed a scribe to issue legal contracts and settle matters of Law.

According to Edersheim, they were self-important. These interpreters of the Law declared that their word was more important than the Law and, among the angels, a single scribe was more highly regarded than all the rest of the people, combined. Jesus' admonitions toward them reflect this level of arrogance.

Were they looking for the Messiah? Their messiah would kick out the Romans and establish the scribes as the elite in government. He certainly wouldn't be a toddler off in some village somewhere.

That could be why no one paid attention when the Wise Men came looking for the King of the Jews. They would wait until he was older and could actually do something before wasting their time chasing some star.

But, when they met Him again thirty years later, they still didn't know Him. He didn't honor them the way they knew the messiah should. He didn't follow their rules like a righteous man ought to, so there's no way this man could be sent from God.

Hope in Hard Choices

Everyone knew Herod's power and what he did to people who crossed him.

Through this fictional account of the scribe, we see the hard decisions people had to face under Herod, and then later under emperors such as Nero. We cannot compromise with evil. It is never satisfied and always wants more.

But, when we stand with Christ, we overcome.

Dig Deeper

Read Daniel 3.

Reread Daniel 3:16-18. These young men, confident in their God, and facing certain death, refused to compromise. They knew right. They chose right. They did right. And God honored them and showed Himself powerful.

Find three more stories in the Bible about people who chose to honor God knowing they would probably lose everything. What was the outcome?

Read *Fox's Book of Martyrs*. What can you learn from the lives of these people who gave their last breath to honor God?

Memorize three promises God gives to people who honor Him. Why did you choose these verses?

You probably don't have to choose between denying God and death, but we are faced with temptations to compromise. In what situations do you find yourself tempted to just let a little thing slide or just stay quiet and not cause a scene?

Sometimes, we aren't sure, but the Holy Spirit gives us boldness. Just like with anything else, we need to start with what we have. If we are only bold enough to say, "God bless you," then we must say it with love and conviction. Soon, we might find the strength to say, "Can I pray with you." And then, "That is wrong." As we exercise the faith given to us, it will grow.

Boldness in Jesus is not license for being rude or disrespectful. We are to always speak the truth in Love.

Pray

Jesus, thank You for being my Strength. Help me walk in the boldness you have given me, and as I do, I trust You will grow my confidence in You and I will stand strong in difficult times.

The Soldier

Hope in the Endless Life

Roman Army Life

WITH ROME TRANSFORMING FROM a Republic to an Empire under Augustus Caesar (r. 27 BC-14 AD), the army underwent a few changes. But largely it continued to operate as it had for almost 500 years and would for the next nearly 500 years.

Discipline was key to army life. Strict discipline created strong soldiers and cohesive units who could dominate the battlefield.

New recruits started in boot camp where intense physical training, long marches, and weapons proficiency prepared them for the disciplined military life.

Early in the Republic era, only citizens could enlist in the army. In the late second century BC, the army shifted from semi-professionals who served for a specific campaign, into a professional, full-time war machine. During this time, non-citizens began being recruited with the promise of citizenship upon retirement. Non-citizens usually served in the auxiliary within their own province. The Syrian auxiliary, which included Judea, was founded in 25 BC.

Structure

The Roman Army consisted of around 50 Legions, led by a *Legatus*. Numbers varied, but generally, each legion consisted of:

- 10 cohorts
- 60 centuries led by a Centurion (6 per cohort)
- 600 Tents (6 per century, 60 per cohort)
- 4,800 men (8 per tent, 80 per century, 480 per cohort)

Legions might be broken up with cohorts and centuries serving in various areas around a region.

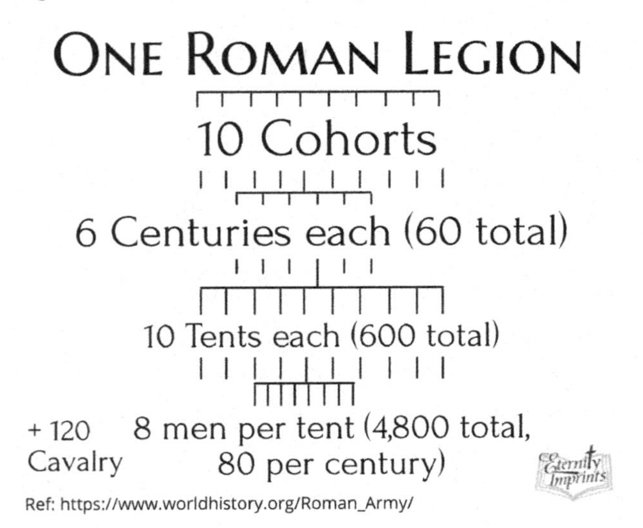

In the Bible

The Bible doesn't talk much about the army, itself. However, several soldiers are mentioned, including:

- The centurion who asked Jesus to heal his servant (Matthew 8:5-13)

- Cornelius, the centurion who called for Peter. He and his household are the first Gentiles recorded as receiving the Holy Spirit. (Acts 10)

- Julius, the centurion in charge of Paul and the other prisoners when they shipwrecked on Malta (Acts 27-28)

- The centurion who took Paul's nephew to the commander with testimony of the plot against Paul, and the troops (two hundred soldiers, two hundred spearmen, and 70 horsemen) who escorted him to Caesarea. (Acts 23:16-32)

The soldier of the Christmas story

The Bible doesn't say there was one. It says:

Then Herod, when he saw that he was deceived by the wise men, was exceedingly angry; and he sent forth and put to death all the male children who were in Bethlehem and in all its districts, from two years old and under, according to the time which he had determined from the wise men. (Matthew 2:16)

Herod sent someone. Bethlehem had about 1,000 residents at the time of Jesus' birth. How many boys under the age of two would be in a population that size? Including the surrounding villages, there probably were fewer than twenty boys. A tax collector, familiar with everyone in the city and already on the Roman payroll, and a handful of soldiers could dispatch that order. But, given the nature of the command, it might take more to ensure compliance.

Was it difficult for the Romans to carry out that order? Officially, in Roman culture, it was considered inappropriate to mourn the death of a child younger than five years old. So, soldiers, who were forbidden to marry and wouldn't have had children, may have held that position. But, we have journals from parents who lost a baby, expressing their frustration and anger that they could not grieve. It stands to reason that, if there were soldiers with younger siblings, nieces and nephews, or unofficial families, they would experience conflict.

In this instance, I chose to humanize the soldiers more than the history books say they should be.

References:

- World History Encyclopedia, Roman Army
- Roman Empire History, Roman Army: Structure, Ranks, Names, Equipment & Facts
- Weapons and Warfare, Roman Auxilia

Hope in the Endless Life

Several times in Jesus' life, men tried to kill Him, but they were never able to. Until the time appointed by the Father. Then, they couldn't take it. He laid it down (John 10:17-18) at the time, in the place, and in the way prescribed by the Father before He laid the foundation of the world.

Then, He shook off death. In His weakest moment, He won the greatest victory, ever. He cannot be defeated.

Dig Deeper

Read Hebrews 7:11-19 (You can read about Abraham and Melchizedek in Genesis 14:18-20.)

The writer of Hebrews is using Melchizedek as a picture of Jesus. Just like Melchizedek was a priest of God, but not under the Law of Moses, Jesus has established a new covenant, not based on endless laws and continual sacrifice, but based on the power of the indestructible life, purchased and proved by His resurrection.

Read Romans 8:35-39. What can separate us from the Love of Christ? There is nothing. Paul says we are more than conquerors. Through the indestructible power of Christ, we cannot be defeated.

Memorize three verses about the victory we have in Jesus Christ. Why did you choose these verses?

How would you live differently if you understood that you cannot lose?

Pray

Thank you, Jesus, for providing my victory. Help me to live in a manner that honors Your sacrifice and shows the world the Hope I have in You.

Joseph, Part 2

Our Eternal Hope

Israel and Egypt

ISRAEL AND EGYPT HAVE a long history together.

Beginning with Abraham, we see him and his descendants look to Egypt for protection during drought and invasions. Sometimes, Egypt serves as an ally, but mostly she is a snare.

- Abraham went to Egypt during a famine (ca 2090 BC) (Genesis 12)

- Hagar, Sarah servant, with whom Abraham had Ishmael was Egyptian. (Genesis 16)

- God told Isaac not to go to Egypt. (Genesis 26)

- Joseph taken to Egypt as a slave but rises to power. (Genesis 37, 39-41)

- Jacob and his family move to Egypt. (Genesis 45-46)

- Israelites live in Egypt for a time, then are forced into slavery under an unknown king who "did not know Joseph." (Exodus 1:8). God hears their cries and frees them. (Exodus 1-14)

- Thirty days after being delivered, from Egypt, the people cried for the security of slavery (Exodus 16). Four months after leaving Egypt, they crafted a calf-idol. (Exodus 32)

- Solomon made a treaty with the king of Egypt and married his daughter. (1 Kings 3:1). Pharaoh gave her Gezer as a dowry. (1 Kings 9:16)

- Solomon imported horses and chariots from Egypt. (1 Kings 10:28-29; 2 Chronicles 1:16-17)

- Egypt was a refuge for political enemies: Hadad and Jeroboam (1 Kings 11, 2 Chronicles 10)

- Wars:

    - Enemies: King Rehoboam and Pharaoh Shishak (1 Kings 14:25, 2 Chronicles 12), King Josiah and Pharaoh Necho (2 Kings 23:29, 2 Chronicles 35:20),

    - Allies: King Hoshea and Pharaoh So (2 Kings 17:4), referenced multiple times in the Prophets

- Pharaoh Necho deposes King Jehoahaz the son of Josiah and installs Jehoahaz's brother Eliakim as king. (2 Chronicles 36:1-4)

- Remnant left from the Babylonian war flees to Egypt where they embrace idolatry once again. (2 Kings 25:26, Jeremiah 42-44)

Our Eternal Hope

Sometimes, God uses unlikely vessels to speak His Truth (Numbers 22:21-39; John 11:49-52). When Sennacherib king of Assyria came against Israel during King Hezekiah's reign, the Rabshakeh said, "Now look! You are trusting in the staff of this broken reed, Egypt, on which if a man leans, it will go into his hand and pierce it. So is Pharaoh king of Egypt to all who trust in him." (2 Kings 18:21) Such Truth spoken by an enemy of God.

But God says, "Out of Egypt I called my son." (Hosea 11:1, Matthew 2:15) We are no longer held by the bonds of slavery and drawn into sin. In Christ Jesus, we have been made free. We have Hope, grounded in the Indestructible Life. It becomes a stabilizing force, anchoring us when life is uncertain. Our circumstances don't define us or our future because Jesus Christ is our Life and Victory.

And that is our True Hope and the real meaning of Christmas.

Dig Deeper

Read John 8:31-59

Reread John 8:31-32 and verse 58. Jesus promises those who abide (dwell, live permanently) in Him will know the Truth and the Truth will *make* us free. Later in the conversation with the

Pharisees, Jesus declares His eternality. "Before Abraham was, I am."

Since Jesus is eternal, existing outside of time, and cannot be defeated, we know that when we are made free by Jesus, we are free for all eternity. We cannot be defeated, and we cannot become a slave again. He is our eternal Hope.

Memorize three verses about our hope in Jesus Christ. Why did you choose these verses?

How does the promise of eternal hope affect your response to challenges in your life?

How can you share this Hope with those around you?

Pray

Jesus, I praise You, my eternal Hope. I am free and walk in victory because of who You are. Teach me to walk in that victory and live in Hope.

The Lord is my shepherd;
I shall not want. Yea, though I walk
through the valley of the shadow
of death, I will fear no evil; For
You are with me; Your rod and
Your staff, they comfort me.
Psalm 23:1, 4

Our Stories

Hope's Fulfillment

Coming Soon!

Sign up for updates at
DeborahGatchel.com

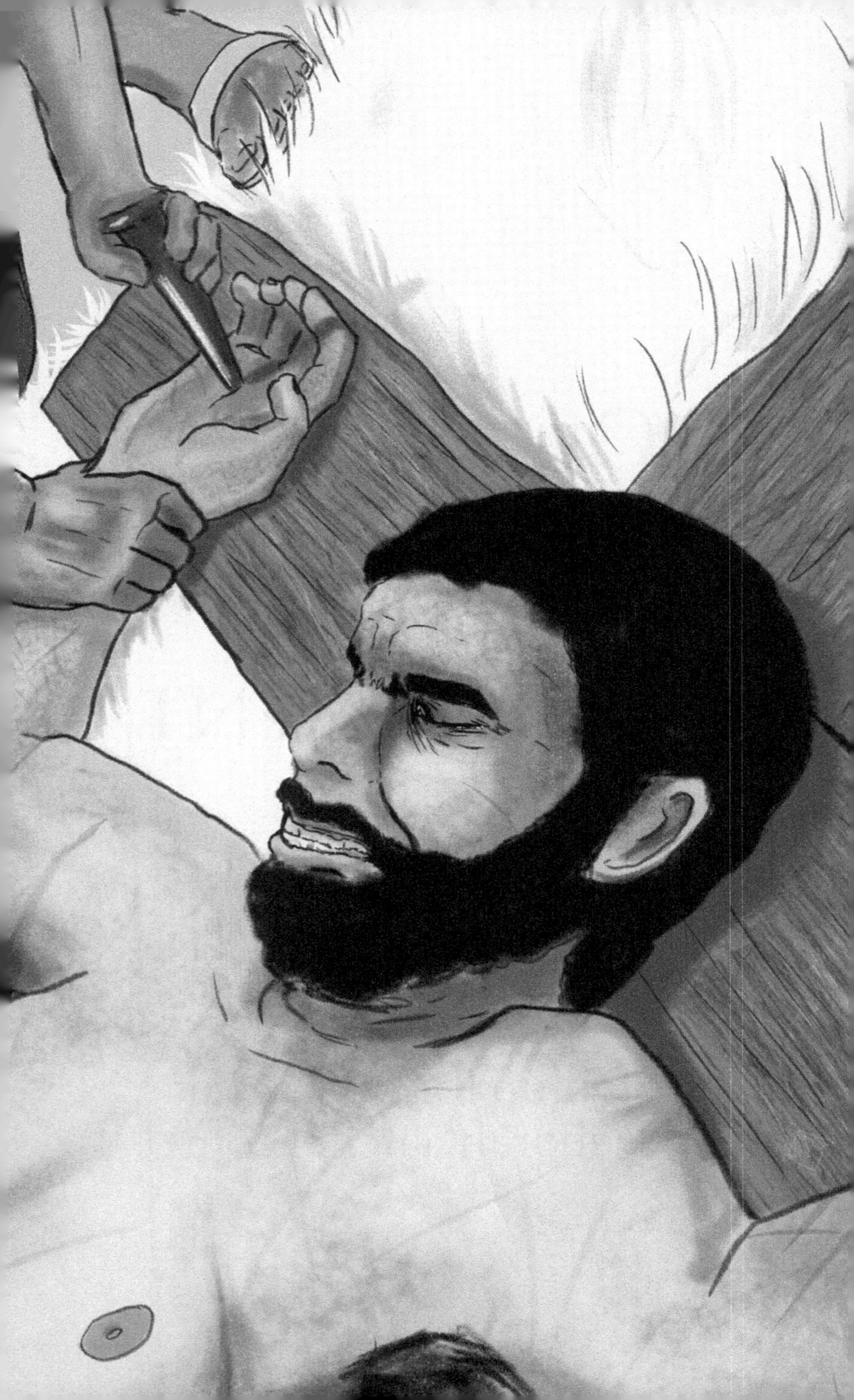

The Thief

I SAT AT THE edge of the crowd in the temple courtyard, listening to the teacher. I laughed when he outwitted the pompous religious leaders. And his story about the two sons tending their father's vineyard. I was the first son. Except, I never went back. *Was it too late? Could I be forgiven?*

Jacob, my boss, knelt beside me and I flinched. I should have been working. I had three more purses than when I started, but, with this crowd and for as long as I had been out, I should have had four times that.

He picked up a pebble and tossed it in the air. "I hear there's a caravan coming from Egypt. They seem quite burdened with all their supplies. Meet me at the Tower of David in two hours. We'll help lighten their load." He stood and turned to go but looked back over his shoulder. "And don't get distracted by fancy words. You have work to do."

I nodded and watched him slip into the crowds. I stepped back to scan for an easy target, but the teacher's story captured my attention, again.

Could I follow him? Walk away from Jacob and start over?

The teacher looked across the crowds toward the collection box and commented on a widow giving her last coins.

At the mention coins, I snapped out of the trance. I glanced at the sun and swore under my breath. I should have been at the tower an hour ago.

I sprinted out of the temple, pushing against the pilgrims trudging up the hill. As I approached the meeting place, I could see Jacob pacing. I skidded to a stop beside him.

He grabbed the collar of my robe and shoved me against the wall. "Where have you been? They're almost here."

I brushed his hands away and shrugged. "But they aren't. We have time."

"Have you studied them? Do you know your target? Do we have a plan?"

I shook my head. "Plan: street brawl. We already have that going. My target: I'll just pick someone. I've done this enough." I started toward the gate.

He grabbed me by the shoulder and shoved me against the wall again. "You can't do that. You'll slip up. They'll catch you. And with a target this size, they'll crucify you."

I laughed and tried to push him away. "So, it's street brawl. Good plan."

He held me tight. "I'm not joking. I'm calling this one off. It's not worth it."

I should have listened. Or maybe I should have walked away to follow the teacher.

Instead, I glanced toward the gate. Half of the Egyptians were already through. I set my foot behind Jacob's and pushed him. He landed on his back. I ran toward the gate, taking in the scene before me. I spotted three purses I knew I could cut. I fingered my knife, getting it into position. My first target made eye contact with me. No good. Two more steps and I was alongside my second target. In one motion, I sliced his purse and side-stepped a dog in my path. As I tucked the purse in my belt, a hand grasped my arm. I tried to twist free, but one of the Egyptians pulled me close to him and held a knife to my throat. I drove my knife into his side and fled.

As I ducked in and out of shops, I heard shouts and footsteps behind me. At the corner, I ran into a stack of grain jars. I leapt behind them just as the soldiers came into view. While they ran by, I held my breath, watching until they turned down the next street.

I counted to thirty. No one returned so I slipped out. My first mistake was not stashing my purses I had gathered. My second mistake was going back to the gate – but I had to know what happened to the man I stabbed.

I didn't see him, but guards ushered the Egyptians through the city. As I turned to slip away, Jacob shouted, "There he is."

I spun around. Two soldiers held him against a wall. I ran, but a group of bystanders wrestled me to the ground. I tried to claim innocence, but they found the purses. I couldn't explain why I would need so many, especially one filled with Egyptian coins.

They put both of us in stocks in the inner prison.

He spent all night cursing me for rushing into the situation. We argued for days until they took us to be whipped – forty less one lashes each. He collapsed at twenty and six. I made it to thirty and two.

The next day they led us out for our final punishment. When the soldier dropped the wooden beam in front of me, I glared at him. He laid his whip across my back. I closed my eyes and picked up the burden.

We started the slow march out of the city: another man in front, Jacob staggering behind me, cursing me with every step.

The man in front stumbled. I lowered the beam to wait for him but was urged on by the bite of the whip across my back. I maneuvered around him as a soldier grabbed an onlooker to carry the fallen man's cross. He stepped in line behind me. At least I didn't need to listen to Jacob anymore.

They drove us up the hill like a line of cattle. Blood ran down my legs as the weight of the beam on my back re-opened my wounds. My mind told me to stop – there was only worse pain at the end of the journey – but the soldier lay the whip deep into my back if I slowed.

The crowds we hailed a week ago for the income we would gain from them, now mocked and spit on us. A few threw stones and rotten food.

When we reached the top of the hill, the guard struck my chest with the handle of his whip and pointed toward the side of the road. I let the burden drop. I wanted to fall to the ground, but I wasn't getting any closer to that thing than necessary. I stood by the side of the road, eyes to the ground.

I heard a scuffle and looked up. Jacob wasn't by his cross. Several paces away a group of soldiers wrestled him to the ground. Two soldiers grabbed his feet and two his arms. They carried him back to his place, slammed him on the beam and hammered his hands in place. He screamed and fought with every blow. As they moved to his feet, the world around me started spinning then went black.

I come to and panic sets in. My clothing lies in a pile at my head. I try to struggle but a soldier pins my right arm against the beam with his knee. Others hold my legs and my other arm. The cold tip of a nail presses against my hand and the soldier raises the hammer. I resolve not to cry out, but as the hammer hits the nail, a yelp escapes. I steel myself for the next blow. They may kill me, but I will not give them the satisfaction of a reaction. I almost break when they drive the nails into my feet. I close my eyes and bite my tongue until they finish.

The centurion reads the sentence of the man beside me, "King of the Jews." I look at him for the first time. It looks like the Romans gave him everything they could. I don't think even his own mother would recognize him. Serves him right – causing trouble with the Romans, proclaiming himself king for us.

They read my conviction, "Murder and theft," and attach the verdict above my head.

The time has come. As a boy, I would watch as they executed criminals. I loved to stand on the side and mock them as they were lifted into place. Once I started working with Jacob, though, I avoided these roads as much as I could. I knew one day....

They lift me and drop me into place. My head jars, my teeth sink into my tongue, and a curse escapes. My struggle for life begins.

I push against the nail in my feet to gasp for air, but the pain is too much so I slump again. The seat is just low enough that the nail pulls at my arms, and I can't breathe fully, but not low enough for me to give up. I push up for another gasp of breath and settle into the rhythm of hanging onto life.

The Jewish leaders gather around the man beside me. One of them calls out, "You saved others. Save yourself so we might believe."

Jacob throws insults at the man. I take a few precious breaths to join in. I know I've done wrong, but at least I never hurt anyone – well except that man earlier this week. But it was an accident. I didn't mean it. He, on the other hand, tried to start a rebellion. Besides, cursing him somehow makes me feel better.

Then he speaks. Softly. I hear the pain in his voice, but no anger. None. "Father, forgive them. They don't know what they're doing."

I know that voice, even through the pain. I look closer and I can see the man he once was – when I was listening to him just a few days ago.

What would have happened if, that day, I had followed him? He's here. Would I still be?

Jacob calls to him, "If you're the Christ, save yourself. And us."

The Christ. Of course. That's who He is. How did I not see?

I look at Him again. He is fighting for breath just like me – but not like me. He isn't angry. He isn't afraid. He doesn't fight back.

Jacob spews more insults. I push up for a deep breath. "What are you doing? We're getting what we deserve, but this Man has done nothing wrong." I take another breath and turn to the Man. "Please, Lord, remember me when You come into Your kingdom."

He looks me in the eye. For a time, the pain is gone. I don't hear the crowds. I see only the Man.

"I promise you, today you will be with Me in Paradise."

Then it all comes back. Nothing has changed. I still am on the cross. I still struggle for every breath.

But everything has changed. I no longer am afraid or angry. How can it be that, in my worst moment, I am most at peace?

Suddenly, the sun darkens as if it's midnight. The crowds scream and the soldiers scramble for torches.

The Teacher calls out. "Father! why have you forsaken me?"

I expect a host of angels to come and rescue Him. Nothing happens.

We fight for life in darkness and silence.

He cries, "It is finished." In the torchlight, I see Him slump forward. An earthquake rattles every bone in my body, tearing my flesh against the nails.

Then the sun appears, and all is quiet.

I wait. Fighting.

They come with the ax to break my legs so I will be dead before the start of Passover. I can no longer push myself up to get a breath. The end is here. My fight is done.

I am ready.

A Note from the Author

Dear reader,

I am blessed that you invested your time reading this story. I trust it was worth your time. I would love to hear from you. Go to DeborahGatchel.com and click on the contact button. Is there anything you thought I missed? What did you find insightful? Who else's story would you like to hear? Is there anything special I can pray with you about? I would love to hear from you.

Finally, don't miss the Scribbles Newsletter. Once a month, I send out a page from my notebook. In *Scribbles Newsletter*, you will:

- Receive a FREE copy of Our Stories: Costly Lentils. Join Esau as he debates with his twin brother over a bowl of stew and a birthright. **Exclusive title for *Scribbles* subscribers.**
- Gain new insights into the Word of God,
- Explore the ways archeology upholds the Truth of scripture,
- Be the first to know about specials and new releases, and

- Keep an open line of communication in case of a glitch in the social media matrix.

Sign up for *Scribbles Newsletter* at
www.DeborahGatchel.com.

Help Others Know What to Expect

Studies indicate that 90% of customers read the comments before they make a purchase. Your honest review will help others know what to expect and help me improve future stories.

Share your experience on your favorite e-book sites.

- What did you like?
- What didn't you like?
- What would you like to see next time?
- Who should read the story?

Your honest review will help. Thank you!

I pray you are abundantly blessed with every spiritual blessing in Christ Jesus.

God is writing YOUR story. Get ready to tell it!

In His Grip,

Deborah Gatchel

Deborah Gatchel
Author, Our Stories

References

BELOW ARE THE GENERAL references I used in researching for this book.

Associates for Biblical Research

Edersheim, Alfred. Temple--Its Ministry and Services Specifically Chapter 8: The Morning and the Evening Sacrifices.

Edersheim, Alfred. *The Life and Times of Jesus the Messiah*, Specifically Vol I, Ch VIII

Jewish Encyclopedia

Jewish Virtual Library

The Red-Haired Archaeologist

Ministry Partners

A huge "Thank You" to everyone who has stood beside to make *Our Stories: Hope's Arrival* a reality.

First, my husband and girls whom I subject to endless archaeology reports and author podcasts.

My mom who is always asking what the next story is and tells me it's amazing even when the first draft is barely readable.

All the people on the Bible Digs Facebook page who patiently answer my impossible questions that I can't find in the above-mentioned reports. (Where would a blacksmith forge be located? What would that pot have looked like?)

Fellowship Writer's Guild for your encouragement and prayers and for your courage to tell me when something didn't work.

My editor and interior illustrator, Christina Gatchel, for making me sound intelligent and bringing the characters to life.

Daniel Cross for lending your historical expertise to help make sure my depictions are as accurate as possible.

Tracy for your patience and brilliance in making my ideas for cover design a reality.

My sister, Dawn, for your help with the book layout.

Those of you who supported me on Kickstarter:

Yadira
Dahlia Martinez
Georgia Thamaravelil
Harbor Parking, Inc.
Harbor Driving, Inc
S & J Weber
Bernabe Martinez
Stan Mack
Jackie M. Oehring
Carol Marhold
Jackson Lindsey

And each of you who pray for me that I have wisdom, creativity, and perseverance.

Dig deeper into historical and cultrual context of

OUR STORIES

HOPE'S ARRIVAL

Go to **DeborahGatchel.com**
Select **blog**, then
A Way in a Manger
or scan the QR Code.

20241022031339